MUSINGS

Musings

An Anthology of Greek-Canadian Literature

EDITED BY

Tess Fragoulis

WITH ASSOCIATE EDITORS

Steven Heighton & Helen Tsiriotakis

Véhicule Press

Published with the generous assistance of The Canada Council for the Arts, the Book Publishing Industry Development Program of the Department of Canadian Heritage, and the Société de développement des entreprises culturelles du Québec (SODEC).

Pan Bouyoucas' "Anna and Sotiris" was first published in French, in his collection of short stories *Docteur Loukoum*, published by Trait d'Union, 2000. The English translation is by the author.
    Margaret Christakos' "Charisma" is excerpted from her book *Charisma*, published by Pedlar Press, 2000. Steven Heighton's "On Earth As It Is" was first published in *On Earth As It Is* by Porcupine's Quill, 1995 and Vintage Canada, 2001. Hélène P. Holden's "Emovora" appeared in *Branching Out*, 1979. Aliki Tryphonopoulos' "Pyreas Point" appeared in *The Backwater Review*, Fall/Winter 1999. Stavros Tsimicalis' poems were first published in the collections *Liturgy of Light*, Aya/Mercury Press, 1986, and *The Fragments*, Porcupine's Quill, 2002. Eleni Zisimatos-Auerbach's "Oracle at Delphi" appeared in *Spire Press*, spring 2003.

Cover design: J.W. Stewart
Set in Adobe Minion by Simon Garamond
Printed by AGMV-Marquis Inc.

NATIONAL LIBRARY OF CANADA CATALOGUING IN PUBLICATION
    Musings : an anthology of Greek-Canadian literature / edited by Tess Fragoulis in association with Steven Heighton and Helen Tsiriotakis.
ISBN 1-55065-186-2
    1. Canadian literature (English)–Greek-Canadian authors. I. Heighton, Steven, 1961- II. Fragoulis, Tess III. Tsiriotakis, Helen, 1967-
PS8235.G73M87 2004   C810.8'0889   C2004-900006-3

Véhicule Press
www.vehiculepress.com

CANADIAN DISTRIBUTION
LitDistCo Distribution, 100 Armstrong Avenue,
Georgetown, Ontario L7G 5S4 / 800.591.6250 / orders@litdistco.ca

U.S. DISTRIBUTION
Independent Publishers Group (IPG)
814 North Franklin Street, Chicago, Illinois 60610
800.888.4741 / frontdesk@ipgbook.com

Printed in Canada

for my grandfather, Constantine Fragoulis

"Everything that any one of us can do to help or hinder his fellow man has been done, at least once, by a Greek."

–Margaret Yourcenar, *Memoirs of Hadrian*

Contents

ACKNOWLEDGEMENTS 10

INTRODUCTION 13

Una McDonnell : *Three Poems* 17

Pan Bouyoucas : *Anna and Sotiris* 22

Antonios Maltezos : *The Naked Companion* 36

Aliki Tryphonopoulos : *Pyraes Point* 43

Tess Fragoulis : EXERPT FROM *Hipster, Hit the Road* 57

Eleni Zisimatos Auerbach : *Three Poems* 73

Stavros Tsimicalis : *Four Poems* 77

Helen Tsiriotakis : *Mr.Frederick and Nancy Drew:*
   The Case of the Vacuum Cleaner Salesman 82

Margaret Christakos : EXCERPTS FROM *Charisma* 92

Steven Heighton : *On Earth as It Is* 109

Hélène P. Holden : *Emovora* 120

Helen Stathopulos : *Two poems* 137

GLOSSARY 143

BIOGRAPHICAL NOTES 145

FURTHER READING 151

Acknowledgements

First and foremost, I would like to thank my associate editors, Steven Heighton and Helen Tsiriotakis for lending their time, opinions, critical faculties, editorial skills and humour to this project; Simon Dardick for seeing the merit of the anthology so quickly and backing it so enthusiastically. For their encouragement and support, Yiorgos Chouliaras and Costas Halavrezos. And Smaro Kamboureli and Martha Klironomos for their interest, contacts, and academic perspective. Finally, I'd like to thank all the writers who submitted their work to the anthology, whether they appear between its covers or not.

Introduction

As a writer of Greek descent, I've been continually frustrated by people's lack of knowledge of Greek culture as it currently exists in both the country itself and its diaspora. In general, readers are very familiar with and interested in the glories of ancient and classical Greece, or in the blue and white Greece popularized through travel and the tourist industry. But even the literary travellers who visit Greece with the noble intention of exploring the land and its culture (and there is a long list of these in Canada alone) tell the only stories an outsider can tell. These revolve around the encounter with "the other" and how this reflects back on themselves and their own culture. Greece then becomes the setting through which we learn about the author and his or her impressions of the landscape and its people, whose inner lives are not readily accessible to the foreigner, and who consequently play the roles of catalyst, obstacle or foil, flitting by as symbols in the peripheral vision of the author.

Unfortunately, authors are often struck by the same sights, the same aspects of social structure, and seem to run into the same types of characters—romanticizing or criticizing them, as required, and delivering a static and often stereotypical Greece. In the end, it is only their personal revelations that are unique. Fair enough. Literature does not necessarily have the same imperatives as social anthropology, nor are such considerations indicative of literary merit. And the popularity of such travelogues is not surprising. Readers identify with the traveller, who is their proxy and their guide, introducing them to the "other" who inhabits this exotic and mythic land.

Identification and recognition are, of course, important elements in the reading experience, and are the second factor in the creation of this anthology. It is true that as a reader I am able to connect psychologically, emotionally and spiritually to worlds very different from my own, and with characters whose paths I might never cross. But my specific experience as a Greek-Canadian has been, for the most part, absent in Canadian literature. Thus I've seldom enjoyed the luxury of immediate recognition that someone native to Southwestern Ontario or Northern Alberta might experience reading about characters living within that specific landscape and cultural reality. There is, I've discovered, a certain level of comfort derived from this recognition and identification which adds another layer to the reading experience.

Going through the submissions to the anthology, encountering the books and poems and stories that my fellow Greek-Canadians had already written in isolation, has not only provided me with this recognition for the first time, but has also placed all of our work within a new context. Many of us are using similar materials and references, drawing from the same pool of cultural signifiers, and traversing a similar cultural landscape towards very different ends.

Whether a Greek-Canadian "voice" exists is a question better left to academics. As one of the anthology's contributors, the elongated perspective necessary to quantify the work and answer this question is not yet available to me. I did, however, notice certain themes and undercurrents which only became evident once the material had been selected and assembled. There is a darkness and urgency in all of the work; where there is humour, it is black or ironic; where there is love, it is sharp, dangerous and consuming. An eroticism is present throughout, even when the work is not explicitly sexual; there is a predisposition towards the mythical, the supernatural, and the magic-real; and there is a fascination with death, especially that of a parent.

Cultural questions aside, the work presented here is powerful, original and exciting—formally, linguistically and in terms of content. *Musings* features writers already established in Canada, brought together as a group for the first time, as well as emerging voices who will surely find a wider audience in coming years. My hope is that readers will be seduced by the darkness, the poetry, the intensity of the work, and startled by its sensory impact. I also hope this anthology will be the first of many encounters with characters and voices that will not only become familiar, but necessary because their company is enticing and worth the journey into a new literary "Greece." A less idealized place, perhaps, but more intimate, real and vital.

Tess Fragoulis

Una McDonnell

Agape

For you I will become the stoneless olive, pulled warm
from leaves, slyly entered and perfectly left: intact

but barren inside the circle. In the dream of a child, the man
looks at the girl with unflinching interest. She will mistake

this for that pull she feels as he winks and strides, lone,
in his own direction. On the road, the roll of tires

hitting gravel and the singe-sound of crickets. She opens
the door, *Efharisto*, steps inside. She is willing to risk the dark

locus of a strange, estranged man—his blood and its pressure
in her veins. *E agape mou yia sena*, she might say, *my love for you,*

the gape of it inside me. Tonight she will sleep inside the moon
of her small silver tent. Pour careful water over hot coal,

watch smoke as it rises, slow, into night—

Desperate Swimmers

(After a mixed media work by Betty Goodwin, *Untitled*, 1994-1995, graphite
and oil stick over gelatin silver print on translucent mylar film, 94 x 71 cm.)

This lone figure floats, face-down
in a subcutaneous sea—
he could be making love, or dead

on a bed of nerves. See how he sinks
when his body longs to be taut?
Taught. Everything we need to know

is held in the body. The skin, a windworn gate-
keeper barring the world from celled
inmates who record our days in their own

arcane language. Our bloody emergence
in the world, penned there, the body
we leave, imprinted. If I could translate

one woman, one man. I write them
in love, if only for an hour.
I am coupled to a drawn man, his death

dance, untold stare in skin and what lies
beneath. I want to open
him, spread him against this graft,

love him nerve-bouncing raw. Doesn't he
know? Don't I? We sink
into our own bodies. He has traded breath

for wisdom: how long can he suppress
breath? How deep is deep enough
in the language of skin? Hours

between two people click past
as cells divide. I will never touch
the hand that touched me first. Never

—like this desperate swimmer:
drowning, dead, or dying
for answers—stop staring into skin.

Grieving Knife

(After a mixed media work by Betty Goodwin, Grieving Knife, 1991, pastel and graphite on translucent mylar film, knife, 85.5 x 71 cm.)

If there is an edge to this, I want to run
my palm along its steel sharpness, let blood
pool and gather until I can float—
an embryo with no cord but my own

small yearning. Somewhere there is an
ancient song. Its rhythms live in skin.
Its slow strum, a choke-throated Ah—
knotted in my tongue, warming words

in my mouth but never speaking.
Will I ever sing me? I have been
given away. Grief follows
the lost child with a stalker's grace.

His knife at my throat, exacting
its price: one family
for another. I take the blade
and in its glint, see my own

fractured reflection. Feel its cold
metal weight in my hand. When I have it,
I use it. With a wretched precision
I tell my first self: You are not real,

of earth, or born. Here, I say.
Cut here. I am
blessedly exact. Conclusions
are satisfying, but bloody.

Anna and Sotiris

I have made up many stories. In this one I relate events exactly as they occurred and every word is true. Yet it is the one story I tell that no one believes.

My mother was born on the Greek island of Leros. She was sixteen years old in 1943 when the Germans bombarded it for forty-one nights to chase the British who had just taken it from the Italians. During one of those nights, to escape the slaughter, my grandparents took their daughter and, as the bombers and fighter planes bellowed overhead, they rowed twenty kilometres to the Turkish coast. Six months later, they reached by land a refugee camp in Palestine where my father, who knew seven languages, was serving his country as an interpreter for the Allied Forces.

By the end of the war, my father and mother had met and married. After the wedding, Sotiris, my mother's father, sailed back to Leros to gather whatever pieces were left of his past. Anna, his wife, did not have the heart to return to the cemetery the island had become after losing, to death and exile, fifteen thousand of its twenty thousand inhabitants. She followed her daughter and her son-in-law, first to Lebanon, then to Canada, to return to Leros fourteen years after she had left it, and only for one month.

I went along. I was ten years old and, thanks to the stories my grandmother had told me, I knew the island and its inhabitants as if I were born there. In fact, because of all the stories Anna told me, to this day, when I think of Greece, I see Leros in my mind's eye, especially the house she had once occupied with Sotiris.

It was in that house that I first came in contact with my roots. It was in that house, many years later, that I came upon the subject of my first novel. It is in that house that I have the most extraordinary dreams. Every night is a festival of dreams, with two or three intermissions to catch my breath. Finally, it was in that house that for the first and only time in my life I was witness to paranormal phenomena.

The house was built on a hill, in the 1860s. Its architecture was typical of Leros: two floors and an inner courtyard surrounded by a wall two metres high. When Sotiris returned to it in 1945, a bomb had demolished part of it and the rest had been emptied of most of its furniture and household items. On my first visit, in 1957, the first floor included the kitchen, the dining room, a maid's room, a living room, a toilet and a storeroom where my grandfather kept his tools, his newspapers and his magazines, his wine and his fishing gear.

On the second floor were three bedrooms. The first two opened on a large terrace facing north, from which you could see the open sea. My grandfather slept in the third room. It had a balcony that faced east. There he drank his coffee every morning, gazing at the rising sun. "Don't talk to me now," he would say. "The world is about to crumble? Let me finish my coffee first."

Sotiris had three sisters. Anna had six brothers. Sotiris and Anna knew each other since childhood. When, at the age of twenty, Sotiris decided to go try his luck in America, he left with Anna's two older brothers. The night before he sailed, he sang under Anna's window until the roosters drowned his voice, swearing that he would return to marry her.

Anna waited eleven years.

During my first night in Leros, I was awakened by my grandfather's voice. He was singing a serenade my grandmother had often hummed to me. *"Open your window, my dove, so I can see your eyes before I die …"*

I got out of bed and looked through the window of my room. My grandparents were seated on their terrace together, for the first time in years, under a moon that took up half the sky. "Do you remember that song?" Sotiris was saying.

My grandmother moved brusquely away as if her husband's breath had scorched her. She could not abide drunks and, since the war, Sotiris always kept a bottle within arm's reach. As she walked away, Sotiris tottered upon his feet and, steeling himself to walk straight, he followed her, saying: "We've had our share of good moments together, haven't we? We've had our share of good moments together?"

Sotiris made numerous other attempts to approach Anna, swearing that he would stop drinking when she would return to live with him. But he always made those promises when he was drunk and all his pleas to win back his wife failed to elicit any positive response. By the end of the week, his attitude changed. Now, every time she would answer one of my questions, he would hasten to taunt her ignorance and give me a different answer.

"What does Leros mean, grandmother?"

My grandmother would answer: "It's a distortion of the word *nero* (water), and in ancient times, the island was called Neros. Because, unlike most Greek islands, it had a great number of springs and brooks and forests. That's why Artemis the huntress, the fierce daughter of Zeus, had claimed it as her domain. One of those springs is still running, a two-minute walk from here, and it still bears the name of Asclepius, the legendary physician and god of medicine."

My grandfather would snort and say: "In ancient times the island was called Kalydna. And it was famous for its large bays, not its bloody springs. It was famous for its strategic location in the Aegean and for its large bays which could hide an entire fleet.

That's why it was always coveted by some conqueror or another. And they came, to stay for a night, a year, or a century, then abandon her, bleeding and mutilated, like a widow who never tried to seduce and whom everyone felt the urge to violate. It was that tragic reputation that one day brought to its shores the apostle John, who was looking for a place in which to settle and write his *Apocalypse*. But he would not keep to his writing. He also wanted to convert the island's inhabitants to his new religion, going on and on about how after death all converts would be sitting on the right side of a gentle and merciful God. He sounded so naive that the islanders decided to sodomize him and thus awaken him to some of life's realities. Outraged, John threw his cloak on the waves and, using it as a raft, floated away, crying back at them: '*Lera!*'— Scum!"

Every morning my grandmother told me the dreams she had during the night, I told her mine, and we spent breakfast interpreting them, for she was convinced that the dead spoke to the living in dreams and omens. After breakfast, during her outings to gather capers, dandelions, mountain tea or—if it had rained —snails, every ruin, every house, every tree and every rock conjured up in her a host of memories and anecdotes peopled with colourful characters and often with their ghosts and spirits. I never tired of her stories and kept asking for more while most boys my age were tearing up their knees on the rocks to reach their favourite diving spot.

When, upon our return, I would repeat to my grandfather some of these stories in the hope of extracting from him some bloodcurdling detail my grandmother might have left out, he laughed at her tall tales, her belief in dreams and, as he called them, her "Oriental" superstitions. "The foolish notions that come to women sometimes!" he would say loudly so that his wife would hear him. "Once this ground is over your head instead of under your feet, all that will be left of you are a few memories in the hearts of the living." To prove his claim, he invited me to spend a night with him at the cemetery. He had done that once, on a dare, with an agnostic friend, he said, to show his fellow islanders that, at night as much as during the day, one should only dread the living.

"We had brought a loaf of bread, a piece of feta cheese, tomatoes, pistachios and wine. When we had our fill, we each laid back on a grave and went to sleep. That night, I got up once—to take a leak. My companion was snoring peacefully. He was no longer snoring in the morning when I was awakened by the song of the birds. He wasn't breathing either. When the doctor arrived, he diagnosed a heart attack and all were convinced that my agnostic companion had been punished for having mocked their loving and merciful God. But when the time came to carry the body to my friend's house for the women to bathe, powder, and dress in its best clothes, we discovered that the material of his slacks was caught on a nail. Like me, he probably wanted to get up during the night to empty his bladder and, in his half-sleep, must have thought that someone was holding him back. Moral of the story: It's within ourselves that the sources of fear lie."

Of course, my grandmother and my mother did not let me spend the night at the cemetery with my grandfather. I went there alone, however, the following morning. I crouched between two graves and waited. There was a breeze, and the sound of the rustling trees slowly grew into voices. One whispered my name. The other said: "Come." I did not run away with fright as my grandmother would have done. I crouched there, steadfast, clenching my teeth and telling myself that it was only my imagination. Thus I took my first step away from Anna's world of magic toward Sotiris's land of rationalism and cynicism.

If Anna noticed a change in me, she said nothing. Only now,

every time my grandfather, sitting in the shade of his vine arbour, held me captive with stories of his voyages, she sent me off to do an errand, giving me extra money to buy myself an ice-cream cone or a comic strip. And when the time came for us to leave the island, she did not give Sotiris a goodbye kiss. When my mother reproached her, she replied that she could never hug, let alone kiss, a lush who reeked of alcohol.

Sotiris's breath reeked of retsina all the years the ground remained under his feet. Eventually, I grew pubic hair, which I found more fascinating than my grandparents. I also had children and it was my turn to take them to see their great-grandfather and show them all the spots Anna had helped me discover and which she herself was beginning to forget.

By the end of the summer of 1975, she seemed to have also forgotten her resolve never to give her alcoholic husband even a parting kiss. She was eighty-three years old. Sotiris was eighty-five. We had carried our valises down to the courtyard and were in the process of bidding each other goodbye when, suddenly, my grandmother hugged her husband tightly and said: "Farewell forever, Sotiris."

The eyes of my mother—their daughter—filled with tears.

My grandfather, without uttering a word, pushed past us and went upstairs to his room.

He died six months later. One night, returning home from one of his jags, he missed a step on his way up to his bedroom. He fractured his hip and when he learned that he would never recover completely, he willed himself to die. Because he loved walking, so much that his shoes turned into slippers. On a whim, he would rove the island any time of the day or night, stopping here and there to smoke a cigarette, relive a memory, or simply count the waves. Anna, too, loved walking, and during Sotiris's last summer,

I saw her stroll up hillsides that would bring her daughter to her knees.

We were in Montreal when Anna learned of her husband's passing. She did not cry. She only said: "Finally, he'll be alone no more."

One year and a half later, when she returned to Leros with my parents, she slipped on the same staircase. At the island's hospital, she refused all food. Seeing her melt away, my mother begged her to eat and stop torturing her. Anna unclenched her teeth once—to tell her daughter: "You're torturing *me*. I'm tired. Let me rest."

A month later, she passed away, on the island of her birth, after living on three continents. And when the time came to bury her, the only plot that was free in the cemetery was the one adjoining Sotiris's grave.

I could not make it to Leros that summer to attend the funeral of the person who had the greatest influence on my life and my perception of women. But four years later, I was at the cemetery at five o'clock in the morning, to partake in the ceremony during which, according to custom, the remains of Anna and Sotiris were exhumed, washed with wine, and placed in the family burial vault. Since then, every time I go to Leros, I start with a visit to that vault. And if I am telling you about it today, it is not to make you believe that the phenomena I am about to describe were caused by my grandparents. I only want to acquaint you with the last residents of the house where these phenomena occurred. Before my grandparents, the house had seen many generations of ancestors. It was even occupied by a German officer during the last two years of the war. But I have only known two of its occupants—Anna and Sotiris. Anyway, I do not believe in ghosts. But I can no longer refute their existence with the same conviction I had before I was witness to these occurrences, however much I would like to deny even what I saw with my very own eyes.

It was the summer of 1983. My parents were already in Leros and when I arrived with my wife and two daughters I found my mother in a dreadful state. "I kept a picture of your grandmother in my bedroom," she said. "But even in the dark, I always had the impression that she was observing me. So last night I took it downstairs to the living room. This morning, the picture was back at its usual place, in my bedroom."

Since my grandmother's death, my mother could not sleep in total darkness, though she suffered from bouts of insomnia. According to my father, her insomnia was a pretext for a nightcap or two because my mother always claimed that whisky helped her relax before going to bed. Thus, rather than take her account of my grandmother's picture seriously, I cautioned her against the mix of alcohol and the terrors of the dark, describing the hallucinations provoked by extreme anxiety and extended periods of wakefulness. For I was sure that she had hallucinated, not when she found her mother's portrait back in her bedroom, but when she thought that she had moved it to the living room downstairs.

A few hours later, my wife was shaking me from my sleep in the middle of the night, whispering into my ear: "There's someone downstairs. I heard footsteps in the courtyard."

I pricked up my ears in my half-sleep.

Nothing. Not even the rustling of the vine and jasmine plants that climbed all the way up to the roof on each side of our window, which we always kept open at night.

"It was probably my mother," I said. "She's moving my grandmother's picture upstairs again to show us in the morning that she was not making it up." Then I shut my eyes, to go back to sleep, when, suddenly, I heard the distinct echo of footfalls in the courtyard. That instantly shook off the last traces of sleep from my mind. There was no doubt about it, someone was walking downstairs. I got out of bed and tiptoed to the window. But as soon as I reached it, the footfalls ceased as abruptly as they had started. I looked down into the yard. There was no one. There was no one on the road that ran alongside the house. I could see that by the gleam of the street lamp. The whole island was asleep.

As I said earlier, all bedrooms were on the second floor. So I concluded that someone had gone down to the bathroom, and I did not think much of the footfalls, even though I had seen no light in the bathroom below. "Whoever it was, he went back to bed," I told my wife as I turned away from the window and toward our bed.

I was about to lie down when the sound of heavy footfalls echoed again in the courtyard. This time, I dashed to the window.

The echo stopped as soon as I leaned out to look below.

"Who's down there?" I said. "Is someone in the courtyard?"

Silence.

I stood there awhile, alert to any sound that was not germane to the night.

Nothing.

"It was probably someone walking by the house, in the street," I told my wife.

"It's a dirt road," she shot back. "That was the sound of shoes on stone paving."

She was right. And the courtyard was paved with flagstones, like an old mosaic. And since the street door was barred, I could only reply: "It couldn't have been a thief. If he'd waited for darkness to jump inside, over a wall two metres high, he'd tread cautiously, not stroll back and forth, tapping his shoes like a bloody flamenco dancer." And I walked away again from the window and toward the bed.

We were sleeping in my grandfather's old bedroom. Therefore we had access to his private balcony. The balcony door was located between the window and the bed, and we kept it shut at night. At the precise moment I was passing in front of it, to reach the bed, making light of my wife's agitation, there was a sound, louder than the crack of thunder and more dreadful than anything I had heard in my entire life. It was not one of those inexplicable sounds of the night, which break upon a profound stillness, rise in the air, linger, and slowly die away. It was a blow, as harsh as if a giant standing on the balcony, on the other side of the door, had kicked its lower panel with all his might.

I stood there stunned, while my wife jolted up, grabbing a lock of her hair to nibble on as she did when she was stressed. However, I managed to recover quickly from my stupor, and five seconds later, I opened the door and sprung out on to the balcony.

No-one was there. There was no wind and the skies were anything but stormy. But even if it had been the wind, the sound would not have been as sharp as a kick. A night bird perhaps? Now and then, in the dark, a bat would crash against the door. But the crash was usually a dull thump, as the sound of footfalls on the dirt road would have been. A rock hurled from the street? There was no rock on the balcony floor.

I spent the rest of the night searching for a logical answer. Pictures formed in my mind, of things I had considered in my childhood and had given up later as ludicrous. I discarded them all, but however hard I tried to rationalize, my wife refuted my explanations one by one, saying: "How is it possible for a living person to enter the courtyard by jumping over a two-metre wall, stroll in the yard, then jump over that wall again, then go round the house, then climb up to the balcony on the second floor, then kick its door, then jump down again from a height of four metres and without breaking a bone, then disappear into the night—all of that in less than two minutes?"

The following day, I did not say a word to my mother about the night's events. It would have only strengthened her belief that the house was haunted. But her curiosity was aroused when I asked everyone if they had gone down to the bathroom during the night. My mother said that she was so afraid that she now kept a night pot under her bed. "But why are you asking?" she said. When my wife told her of the sounds we had heard, she almost fainted. To reassure her, I told her about auditory hallucinations and the conditions that are most favourable for their occurence: when falling in and out of sleep one's level of attention begins to subside and can no longer protect consciousness from the intrusion of unconscious thoughts; dreams that continue into wakefulness, which frequently occur when one is still in bed and his consciousness is still impinged upon by unconscious thoughts. These were explanations meant to reassure me as much as her, though I was not alone when I heard the sharp, distinct and rapid sound of footsteps in the courtyard. If my wife and I were still half-asleep then, we were certainly wide awake when we heard the battering ram sound that had so violently shaken the door of the balcony. At that very moment, I had even felt the presence of someone or something outside, separated from me only by the door. I knew all this, yet I kept rationalizing and repeating that there had to be an explanation.

I was still searching for one that evening when I joined my mother in the kitchen. She was making a pot of mountain tea because, she said, she would not sleep a wink even if she emptied a whole bottle of whisky. My wife joined us after she put our daughters to bed, on the second floor.

My mother kept jumping at the slightest sound, and I laughed at her as my grandfather had once laughed at my grandmother.

My mother scowled. "What more will it take for you to believe? Even idiots yield to such hard evidence."

"He's an intellectual," my wife said. "He can't abide the obvious."

"I was at my mother's bedside when she passed away," my mother went on to say. "She'd melted like a candle. The last days, she couldn't even see me. Yet she kept her eyes wide open, and looked, with a smile, to the left, then to the right, as if a crowd had gathered around her bed. And now and then, she'd say: 'Yes, father.' 'I'm coming, mother.' 'Where's Sotiris? How's he doing?'"

"Hallucinations," I said. "Hallucinations and imaginings of a fevered mind."

To cheer her up, I decided to tell her about the night my grandfather had spent at the cemetery with his agnostic friend. I had hardly started when, suddenly, an object fell between our cups of mountain tea.

It was a set of old dentures.

There was a moment of silence, then we looked up at the ceiling. There was no hole where the false teeth could have been hidden, not even a nail to hang them on. Anyway, who would keep his dentures four metres above ground? Even if someone was crazy enough to do that, how come no one had ever noticed the dentures, especially the house painters who whitewashed the walls every two years? Yet those dentures had fallen on our table from the ceiling. And when my mother put on her reading glasses to examine them, she said, stifling a cry: "They're my father's. He only used them when we had meat."

I would have never believed it had I not seen it with my very own eyes. Come on, a set of old choppers, and my grandfather's choppers to boot, falling from above, at the very moment I was about to tell of his night at the cemetery? What, he was eavesdropping on us and wanted to signify to me that he was wrong twenty-five years ago when he claimed that the dead are nothing but dust and memories? Fortunately, I had two witnesses. And all three of us were well awake and drinking mountain tea.

There were no other occurrences that summer. My three subsequent stays in that house also passed without incident. I must add, however, that these were short visits of four or five days, and that my mother had undertaken major renovations to render the house less "depressing." My father had retired and she wanted to spend more time in Greece. Thus, my grandfather's storeroom was converted into a modern bathroom, and the crazy paving of the courtyard was covered with cement, as was the second-floor balcony and the terrace. There were changes on the island as well. Everyone acquired a car or a motorcycle, and many had both. This led to bulging waistlines in a once hardy and slim race of sailors and fishermen. And since there were no sidewalks, you kept checking over your shoulder wherever you walked. "Do you have to walk everywhere?" my mother would now tell me. "Take a taxi now and then. What will people think?"

Upon my return from my last trip, I met my sister's son in a café on rue Bernard to show him the pictures I had taken. He had not been to Leros for several years, and together we lamented over the changes, especially my mother's renovations. To "brighten up" the house, not only had she paved the courtyard with cement, she had also uprooted the vine and jasmine that her father had planted there after the war, to see life grow and blossom again in his house. The vine had reached his private balcony, covering it like a canopy. The jasmine had reached the roof, on the other side of the house, and every night, its heady fragrance blended tenderly with the sea breeze, transforming the terrace into a flying carpet gliding under the firmament. Because at night, when all the lights are out, the sky of Leros is still the most star-studded I have ever seen. And however much I distance myself from it, like my grandparents it will continue to glitter in my memory, for it has etched its mark in the very core of my heart.

"Have I told you what happened to me on that terrace, in 1984?" my nephew said. "I was spending the summer in Leros with my parents, and slept in the room you occupy when you go there."

"Sotiris's room."

"I saw him only once—in 1975—and I was one and a half years old. In 1984, I was ten, and I often sleepwalked. One night, I got out of bed, opened the door of the room and went out on the terrace. Everyone was asleep. I was asleep, too, and not aware of what I was doing. Suddenly, I saw Sotiris—there, in front of me, on the terrace. He said: 'Where are you going, my child?' I woke up and found myself standing on the terrace's parapet. It was as thick as the walls of the house—at least fifty centimetres. Still, one more step and I'd have sleepwalked over that parapet to my death."

Antonios Maltezos

The Naked Companion

Sophia carried the naked creature all the way to the coastal village.
She stopped people on the esplanade, people she normally
wouldn't speak to. She demanded to know who would do this to
an old spinster woman? She held him up for everyone to see: in
the cafés where the men played with their dominoes; in the tavern
where the fishermen ate part of their catch and sipped their liquor;
in the shops where women collected things for their homes, where
they gossiped. Some people called her crazy, others laughed. She
almost threw him into the sea then, and would have had he not
been so obviously hungry. She tried to soothe him with some
words, sounds, and then realized he needed a name. She called
him Pandelis before strapping him on her back for the long
journey inland. It was her father's name, the only man she could
truthfully say she ever knew.

She remembered when the land belonged to her father. It was
sectioned off then. The pigs always lived where the earth was
slightly sunken, where the pistachio trees have now grown thick.
She never went there as a little girl, and her father never forced
her. *I don't ever send you to the pigs, do I? Do I? But I do expect you
to feed the chickens...when I don't have time.* He was a good father.
He even let her feed the chickens from her bedroom widow high
up on the second floor. He watched her while urinating at the
center of the pig's enclosure, his back to her, his neck twisted so
he could smile up at her. She held her hand out over the sill, her
tiny fingers barely able to contain the little hill of dried corn. The
chickens fought for each giblet as it fell tumbling out of the sky.
And she watched, mesmerized, as the hill slowly disappeared.

Only then did she peer over the sill at the action below.

I don't ever send you to the pigs, do I? She remembered the smile, that loving smile, but she replaced his voice with her own because she couldn't hear it anymore. It seemed lost to her forever.

She tried to suckle Pandelis his first day home, but nothing came out. He wailed from hunger and she pulled at her nipples, but nothing came. When her breasts started to ache, she ran outside to fetch some goat's milk.

Pandelis gagged and spat out the milk when Sophia tipped the bowl into his open mouth. He seemed angry then, biting at the air as if trying to fill his mouth with one of her exposed breasts. In a panic, and not knowing what else to do, she poured some of the milk onto her breast. She leaned forward so that Pandelis could reach it. He sucked furiously at first, as if she might have deserved it for teasing him. "Lick at it, you little devil," she implored, and he did, catching every drop with his tongue. She had to pull back from time to time because little Pandelis' mouth was full of teeth.

As a child, she spent most of her time between chores sitting like a sentry at her window, mesmerized by the waves of heat that swirled the earthen tones of the naked and distant landscape. Sometimes she looked down at the chickens and laughed as they tried to get at feed fallen in cracks and crevasses. Sometimes, though, if her father was off somewhere, she became preoccupied by the open space that lay between her home and the horizon.

She had seen her father cross that landscape a thousand times. Her eyes burned from the dry heat, but she never lost the focus needed to watch him disappear. There was some sadness, of course, because he meant everything to her. He always wanted to know where she was and what she was doing, unlike her mother who was always looking down at something, her hands busy, her face contorted.

Sometimes, Sophia slipped out of her window and soared on

the updrafts, the heat as it trembled upwards. She would swirl into nothing, dipping down into those earthen tones and then rise up again—all the while spying her father on his great adventures.

She slept well most nights with little Pandelis at her side. But at other times, she would dream about that figure in the pistachio trees. She thought it must be a young woman because she could clearly make out the pink of flesh amidst the black trunks. It was a trollop sow come to spy on Sophia. Let her spy if she wants, Sophia would say to herself just before her morning prayers.

On days when the chores were light, Sophia placed a chair by the window on the second floor so that she and Pandelis could look out across the land. She told him how her father always returned from his long walks with his pockets full of pistachios, his skin a little darker, his teeth a little whiter.

She loved the way he came into the house, too tired to even look at the enclosures, the livestock. She could always tell by the expression on his face, the way he sat at the kitchen table, that his belly was full. Her mother always tried to ruin the moment with her worry. She was afraid the sun would boil his brains. She would implore him to plant his own trees, and he would drown out her voice by emptying his pockets of pistachio shells onto the kitchen table. Sophia would laugh out loud and her mother would become upset, slipping into her usual tirade.

"They'll find you dead half-way home, or mad from the heat, lost like a fool too drunk to find his way home."

Little Pandelis seemed to enjoy sitting with Sophia by the window. He would recline lazily between her breasts, his head tilted to one side, listening to the sound of her voice as he occasionally adjusted his warmth in her lap. It was during one of these dreamy occasions when both Sophia and Pandelis were startled by the sound of a snapping branch.

Pandelis sniffed at the air, strained his neck trying to look out over the sill as Sophia held him tight. She knew who it was. She whispered a curse as she began to massage her breast through her shirt, squeezing at the nipple at the end of each caress.

It was the young woman from her dreams. She was squatting behind one of the pistachio trees Sophia planted when her father disappeared. She watched intently as the figure ran hunched over behind another tree. What a silly place to hide, she thought to herself.

They never found her father's body, not that anyone really looked. The young still sing about crazy Pandelis come to steal your pistachios in the night.

Sophia was getting angry. "I'll put you with the pigs," she called out, and then she thought that maybe she should run outside with one of her knives, chase the trollop sow down.

When it was time, her father would choose a pig, twist its ear with a powerful hand, force it to follow him to the house where he would call out to his wife.

Sophia always believed that some part of her mother enjoyed the slaughter, but that was only because it meant there would be one less pig to stink up the air.

Thankfully, Sophia was already a mature woman when her mother died. She grieved for a while when she first realized there would be no one to talk with anymore, not at home, not in the mornings or late afternoons. It was the animals who brought her to her senses with their cries for food. And then she became her father, urinating in the mornings among the pistachio trees where the pig's enclosure was, forgetting the years she spent alone with her mother, forgetting the pledge they made. Sophia was going to plant her trees, and together they were to clean the area, sell the pigs one by one.

She planted the trees, but the smell of urine permeated the

earth. Her closest neighbors blamed her for the smell that drifted across their landscape, and she realized the extent of her father's isolation. They scowled at her when she went to market. She was told the meat she was peddling stank of urine, so she abandoned the idea of getting rid of the pigs. And the trees grew tall and heavy with pistachios, marking the many years she struggled with the land all alone.

The only thing she could truthfully say she occasionally yearned for was the watermelon man she remembered from her youth. Her father always bought two of the biggest from the cart. He would call Sophia down from her room so she could see him carrying the two big beasts on his shoulders.

Sophia held on tight to Pandelis, straining her ears, wishing she could hear her father calling her down to the kitchen one last time.

The figure among the trees frightened her. Maybe that silly woman wanted to steal some nuts? Well, she could have them all if she wanted, if she could stand the smell.

"I've pissed on them all," she called out, and a hundred figures seemed to stir all at once.

Pandelis' head bobbed up and down, as if he were sniffing at each and every one of them.

She saw that movement, but she was lost in thought. What was it her father used to say about the earth? If only she could remember the sound of his voice, then his words might come to her.

Pandelis started to squirm, so Sophia pulled one of her breasts out of her shirt. She squeezed it, sending a jet of milk over Pandelis's head. He closed his eyes and reached for it with his open mouth, his two front teeth scraping the soft flesh above the nipple.

She didn't want trouble, especially from the people who lived in the coastal village. The woman hiding in her trees was probably from the coast. In fact, she was certain it was a coastal villager who placed Pandelis at her doorstep. Not that she minded anymore, but still, it was a cruel thing to do to an old spinster woman.

Sophia would make due, though, if only they wouldn't interfere. She didn't want anyone interfering now. She didn't want anyone telling her how to raise him. She rehearsed what she would say. Pandelis had been forced on her, and it was enough that she filled his food bowl daily. It was enough that she allowed him to sleep in her bed.

What was it her father used to say?

There is a right way and a wrong way to prepare the earth for the pigs.

Sophia spotted the woman poking her head out from behind the pistachio tree. She was staring up at Sophia as more of them started to show themselves, stepping away from their hiding places.

First, you've got to lay down the scraps.

Sophia realized her father was talking to her. She recognized the voice, the baritone rasp, the sound of his big teeth chewing on each word.

But this is an island where the air is thick with salt and the sun is always burning down on our heads.

Pandelis bit down on Sophia's nipple. She yelled as loud as she could because the pain was unbearable, and still her father's voice came back to her.

In this dry climate, Sophia, it's a struggle to keep the earth moist. Promise me you'll take care of the land when I'm gone.

Her father had been so proud of that slop-heap, the way the flies bounced off the steaming mass in the mornings. Sophia could smell it now, the way her neighbors probably smelled it then. Still, she loved her father, and missed him terribly even after all these years. But the smell was unbearable, and the only way she could escape it was by placing herself above the stench.

Sophia, my sweet little Sophia! Come down and see what I've got for you.

The smell down there would absolutely spoil the treat for her. Only her mother's understanding expression soothed the little girl's torment.

The sow was making noises, a cruel kind of laughter, and Sophia became enraged, pushing Pandelis off her lap. She stood up and leaned out the window, her large breast like the evil eye.

"Back to the sea, you bastards."

They laughed as Sophia howled. And then they became hysterical when they saw Pandelis push open the front door with his nose.

He ran straight into the crowd because that was where the earth was sunken, where the pigs lived.

Pyraes Point

Manos Natreus lived three flights up from me in an apartment overlooking the Aegean Sea. My parents' apartment gave out on a steep, rocky barren, where a scrawny pine forest used to be until some developers set fire to it in the night. Manos had three older sisters who were all married, and who came over occasionally to spoil him with gifts and candies. When I went up on such days, we would wait until the conversation really started, then we'd milk our water glasses with a little ouzo and enjoy one of his father's cigars on the balcony. Sometimes, I had cards of movie stars from my father's business trips to Athens, and we would play *tavli* until Manos owned my cards, or, less often, until I went home sour-breathed from candied almonds and *loukoumia*.

The town we lived in during the summer was very small—if it could be considered one at all. Two hundred summer homes strung along a seafront road. There was a small strip of seasonal motels along the northern beach, a grocery, a convenience store, Assimopoulos's over-priced restaurant, and the jigsaw fitted apartment block where Manos and I lived. It was not a place where tourists stayed long after they'd seen the Temple of Poseidon.

Old Theo was having his roof rebuilt. His son owned the sole restaurant and grocery, and charged so much that only the tourists stopped there. The Assimopouli seemed to have plenty of money to squander on ornamental tile driveways and pissing lawn fountains.

We sat in the shade of a few scorched cypresses and watched the leathery workmen on the roof across the road. It was a slow day, and the view was not hugely interesting, but we were feeling lazy in the resiny scent of the trees. It was too hot to ride bikes for a few hours yet. At lunchtime, Old Theo came out and told the men to come down and eat. He had a veranda overlooking the Mediterranean on the other side of the house.

Manos decided that we should climb up to the roof and investigate the workmen's progress. We scuttled over the roof and crouched at the other side until we were sure that everyone (including Angeliki, Theo's nutty old wife, who was always leaving fruit offerings at the roadside shrines) was sitting out back, chewing to the drone of the cicadas. We knew that if they listened to that monotonous music long, they would have to siesta. We wandered back over the roof and inspected a skylight that was being fitted.

"Look at that," Manos exclaimed. "So God can see them going kaka!"

I went over and looked. Soon I found myself covering the window with little pebbles that were scattered about the roof.

"Have some respect, Assimopoulo!" Manos muttered, as he started to paint the window with a black, tarry substance that stank and constricted my lungs.

Outdone, and a little annoyed, I went over to the chimney to see if there was anything that needed work. It looked grimy, and too small to fit into. I could see myself getting wedged in there until Old Theo lit his first winter fire. In the drowsy, white heat, I began to entertain apocalyptic scenarios: how my parents would behave if the fire department had to rope me out by the feet, withered, blackened, and incapable of finishing the semester. Yes, but it would have to look like an accident. Maybe they would even forgive me for losing my 18 karat gold cross in Patriots Gardens when I was eight.

I heard the sound of brittle substances rubbing against each other, like clay pots filled with earth being dragged across a patio. Manos let out a little "*opa!*" and I turned to see him fall, belly-first, through the roof. Fired clay and plaster exploded on the hard floor and porcelain below.

I scrambled as near to the hole as I dared. Lying on my stomach, I inched forward to the crumbling edge.

Manos was lying beside the bubble skylight, half black with tar and powdered with plaster. There was a mass of rubble around him. A crayon-sized gash above his left brow leaked blood. One of his arms was tucked up in a way that no normal shoulder would permit. His eyes, full of reproach, met mine. "Make a distraction, Aleko," he said. "Zoë's."

Zoë was the proprietress of the convenience store. Our reconnaissance missions usually ended there with an Italian imported ice cream—the big ones that came in paper-wrapped cones with names like "Chicago" and "All-Star Fudge."

I didn't know what distraction to make, so I hurried to the edge of the roof, overlooking the veranda, and started to whistle. No one was there. It took a moment for my wits to catch up with me. I ran to the ladder and checked to see if it was safe to climb down. Shrieks and saintly names were issuing from the hole in the roof.

One of the workmen ran out and spotted me. I was scrambling back up the ladder, but he caught me by the sandal and pulled with a vengeance. My chin cracked off of one of the rungs on my way into the big man's arms.

Manos's parents have always been better people than my own. Manos said his mother slapped him once in the hospital and has been feeding him *galaktaboureko* and syrup-soaked cookies ever since. He said he heard his father laughing as he recounted the story to a nurse. When I cautioned my father about the possibility of my having a fractured jaw, he slapped me and then strapped my back and legs with his widest dress belt.

But all of these injustices were trivial. They were nothing compared with the supreme humiliation of being volunteered as Old Theo's gardener for the rest of the summer. I was to pick diseased apricots and twine Angeliki's hunchbacked tomatoes while Manos drank *lemonathes* with his arm on a pillow and the T.V. pulled out on the balcony.

When I wasn't spending my mornings over at Theo's, I was "at the pool." My mother imposed this fate on me, since she thought Manos inspired my misdeeds. (Manos and I had worked it out that we would blame each other in cases like this, but I didn't expect a remedy like separation.) At first, I really did go to the pool, where I played idiotic racing games with the younger kids. Fortunately, the pool is not visible from our balcony, and though my mom checked on me the first few days, unexpectedly bringing me a hat for the sun or a few drachmas to pick up some bread from the store, the impromptu visits ceased when my aunt arrived for a week.

Manos and I met for the first time since the incident down at Zoë's. Neither of us had any money for ice cream, and since we'd been caught stealing before, we didn't think we would stretch Zoë's patience so far that she would have to call our parents.

"When my dad took me to Athens last week, there was this American *manouli* more *komati* than the Beouf-alo jeans girl. If I hadna' had to come back, we'd a done everything instead of just kissing and feeling."

I wondered how Manos could have felt anything with his arm in that zeppelin. We were sitting on the padlocked freezer at the back of the store, chewing the thimbleful of tobacco that Manos had managed to nick from one of his brothers-in-law.

"I'll believe that when Dhora looks at you with two eyes."

Dhora couldn't look at anything with both eyes.

"All right, Alekaki. I was down at the north beach yesterday and there's some *manoulia* from Britannia staying there. A whole flock of them. I say the first one to get it going with a British *manouli* gets the next ten ice creams free. And Aleko, *paidaki mou*, it won't be you!"

I had to admit that even with a cast on his arm and glossy, black stitches in his head, Manos was in a better position to succeed. Where I excelled at academics, football and swimming, he could make people laugh and smother him with affection. It helped that he looked young for his age, with long limbs and the skinny, hairless body of a ten-year-old girl. His hair was curly and coarse as a goat's, and he had a rose in each cheek. Old people mistook his fat-lipped smile for cuteness, but I knew it to be flatulent arrogance. I revelled in the secret knowledge that I would, as my mother had assured me time and again, grow into my looks, while Manos would become an overgrown abomination of himself. No, I would never be delicate or cute. I was already getting a *moustaki*, and my voice was safely beyond the cracking stage.

I didn't think I could get the girls' attention, at least not in the right kind of way, but I wasn't going to let Manos languish in his donkey-assed lies.

"All right, *Erotiari*. Lead the way."

When we arrived at the north beach, there was no sign of any British ducks. We were too disappointed to settle for sneaking sidelong glances at the topless mothers we knew by Christian name. It was too hot for that, and neither of us had brought our sunglasses. Manos spotted little Andreas, and we nipped under the peppermint-swirl of his umbrella. We would have rolled him out onto the scorching sand, except his parents were sitting under the family umbrella a few metres away. Mrs. Donakopoulos was already fixing us with her look. She was such a gossip, she would have heard about Theo's before it happened. I didn't care, though, because I knew she stole towels from the church after service. Every time we cycled past her house, there were a dozen white hand-towels on her clothesline, flapping in the wind for all to see.

We made huge grins at the brat, settling close on either side of him. He was forever trying to tag along on his one-speeder when we rode past his house to the burial ruins. He was like a dog too dumb to learn.

Now he was talking so fast that his face began to look crazed for air. Something about new snorkelling gear and his name day.

"Never mind that Andre mou, where are the British *manoulia*? You know, the *touristes* who were here the other day."

Andreas's mouth hung open. I frowned at his almond-shaped skull.

"They're watching Stavros dive. Saw 'em on the way down. But guys, let's go swimming. You can be sharks and I'll be Cousteau who is diving to see the little fish. Then you guys can…"

"Andre *mou*, where's Stavros?"

"I'll show you." He was already pushing on his flip-flops.

"No, Andrea, you stay here with your parents." Manos was pressing his fingers into Andreas's soft, sunburned shoulder, where it was already scar pink.

When he started to cry out, Manos dropped his arm around the whiner and pretended to wrestle with him.

"Mama! Ma, I'm going to get an ice cream with Mano and Aleko," Andreas bawled.

"Be quick! You watch out for him, you two. I mean it. He's younger than you…and don't cross the highway!"

Manos gave me a dark look as we headed towards the pathway, Andreas making double-time beside us, his snorkel bouncing around his neck. As soon as we reached the tree-lined path, we grabbed him. I locked his hands behind his back and Manos yanked his ear to his shoulder.

"You did that on purpose, *mikri pordi*. Where's the *touristes*?"

"At Pyraes Point! Pyraes Point!" Andreas yipped, his face flushing with blood.

We let him go and shoved him back down the path.

"Tell your mom that Zoë's is out of ice cream. Avocados like you shouldn't eat it!"

We set off towards Pyraes Point, Andreas following at a distance. Whenever he came into range, we pushed him back. He started a chant about Ellas being a free country, just to be sure we couldn't forget about him.

The path finally opened onto the flat land of the ridge. I saw Stavros preparing himself in the distance at the edge of the cliff.

"There he is!" shouted Andreas.

"Shut up, beast!" Manos hissed, swatting him back. "You stay here and don't follow us. Or Aleko will throw you to the sharks."

Some of the young women who had been watching Stavros glanced at us. They were at least five years older, and showing a lot of skin. We sauntered over as best we could. I felt oddly insubstantial, like I didn't have sufficient body weight to carry myself like a man. The girls were mainly tall, with small, rounded features. They looked away.

Stavros paid us no attention, and neither did the most beautiful woman I had ever seen outside of the movies. She was standing closest to him, watching as he raised his arms over his head and paused in a pillar, the sun drying the water on his thickly muscled back. All this hamming was redeemed when he threw himself out over the sea and fell from our sight. Even Manos stepped to the edge to witness his entry thirty metres below.

"Work horse," he muttered.

The young women turned toward themselves, exhaling,

smiling, shaking their heads. They said some words that I recognized (although English was a class I freely skipped). Christ! Bly me! Oily sheet!

The beautiful one stepped to the edge again to watch Stavros swim along the base of the cliff. She had hair that was three different colours and twisted up in gnarled bunches like a messy Cleopatra. She was wearing a silver bathing suit with plastic windows in it. There was a tattoo of fireworks exploding on her ankle. I stared at her obliquely, prickly torment setting my flesh in bumps, dampening my hands and feet.

It is common to see beautiful people in the movies and to collect them on cards, but they had never been flesh inhabitants of my world. When I locked glances with her for a second, I felt like I had been dropped into the centre of a stadium filled to capacity, my body indecently normal, my mind a flashflood of astonishment and shame. I felt devastated by the fleeting proximity of a world where things were greater—more important and beautiful—than anything I would ever own or touch.

Andreas had gone further up the plateau and was lobbing stones into the sea. I suddenly wanted to throw stones, too. Big ones. I wanted to whip them out over the sea, hurling out my frustrations with each organ-sized rock: too young, too mute, too ugly....

I glared out at the water. I didn't notice Manos approach the beautiful Cleo until his voice, soft and faintly obscene when he spoke English, reached me.

"Stavros is not a happy man. He not likes the women," he pronounced gravely, glancing towards the opening of the path, as though Stavros could have cheated time and been at the top already.

The women gave him incredulous looks. I couldn't see where

this was leading, aside from a trouncing. I was in the grips of a black humour and wanted to leave.

"This water is very... much. Any man can jump this water. But up there...not much water. Me and Aleko jump there often. You see. Come see him. Yes?"

The women were laughing.

"What are you talking about, *re malaka*? First you call Stavros a queer—he'll crack you like a walnut if he finds out—and now we're gonna jump off cliffs so we can get applauded to our graves?"

"Listen, Alekaki. Listen!" He looped me in conspiratorially with his good arm. "This part up here is actually deeper than where Stavros dove. I know 'cause I've snorkelled it. I'm counting on you, Aleko—I'd jump, but how am I s'posed to swim with this tank? Come on...I bet they'd let us take them for a drink."

Manos had been leading me in the direction of the "shallower" water. Andreas, already bored with his rocks, intuited an intrigue and was staring.

"No chance! I've never dived from anything this high."

"It's no different than the diving-board at school. You're just in the air a little longer. Falling's no work...I'd be in the water right now if I didn't have this stupid cast. I'd back-flip it if I knew how. You gotta do the twist dive! I bet that bull-necked Stavros couldn't do that. But hurry, for God's sake! Before he gets up here and sees us stealing his grapes."

"Is he gonna jump or what?" one of the *manoulia* asked impatiently, blowing air out of the side of her mouth. She was the wart of the group, with orangey hair and freckles that were peeling away on her nose and shoulders to reveal skin the colour of an unripe *karpouzi*. I imagined how that flesh would feel impacting on the water, and smiled.

I suddenly noticed Cleo watching me. My body straightened involuntarily. She was standing apart from her friends, in the same spot where Stavros had jumped. I thought she was shivering slightly, but it was hard to tell. Her mouth looked as if it wanted to smile, but was waiting for instructions. I felt my own cheeks set in prune-sized knots. Her friends had gone back to talking among themselves.

I didn't have vertigo, but looking down at such a drop, I felt the fear of an unexpected push. I tore open the velcro on my sandals. The girls looked over again. Staggering my feet, I studied the sheer wall of the cliff until I could close my eyes and see its afterimage. I turned my back to it and faced the crowd, pulling off my shirt so I could avoid their faces for few more seconds.

"That's it, *Erotiari!* The twist dive now and you'll be the new pinup boy!"

When I raised my head towards the sky, the day filtered prematurely crimson through my lids. If Stavros reached the upper ledge, I would not jump. I was terrified of his halting shout; I waited for it. I could hear Andreas's demented *pida, pida, pida, pida.* The pattern of the shore below was still etched in negative. I fluttered my eyes open again and caught Cleo over Manos's shoulder. Her body was turned to the sea, but she was waiting for my lead. I rolled my head from side to side, raising my arms. Before I could delay longer, my body sprang backwards, spiralling with the motion of my head. By the time I reached the water, I had a terrific charley horse in my calf.

The skin of the sea clubbed my head with such force that I thought it had burst open like *mousmoula* under a pestle. It clapped its palm against the underside of my body, exploding there. My eyes clenched against the mean chill. I began to slow myself, spreading out my arms and legs. My ears were plugged, cramping inward on my paper skull. I arced up to the surface as straight and true as I could with the brick in my calf.

From above, I saw—before I heard—Manos cheering, his

silhouetted form pointing towards the outcropping of rock where I could swim to the path. I awkwardly massaged my muscle to one third of its size and glided gently towards the outcropping, allowing the water to fight me towards the wall of the cliff. I had to use some energy to navigate a safe distance from a jellyfish. My head throbbed. My chest felt as if it had been squeezed like market fruit in the hands of an old *yiayia*.

I felt the sudden, sobering conviction that my parents would come to know of this—if not through a report from Stavros, then from rousing me to demand an explanation when I bled out my organs that night. I was beginning to feel miserable and penitent. All they wanted was for me to grow up in the likeness of a well-formed man, with common sense enough to be a physician or an architect. I began to feel ashamed at having flung their hopes over a precipice for the attention of some *touristes* who wouldn't even remember who I was tomorrow. In fact, they would have had a better story to tell if I had impaled myself on a crag.

As I swam round the curve of the cliff, I found Andreas already waiting, observing me through his snorkel. Stavros was a few metres beyond him, quickly navigating the last large rocks. I felt an awful fear when I saw him. He would tell. Was he not a bartender? The whole thing was ugly—ugly and awful and, truly, more than half Manos's fault.

The women were still some ways up, descending as quickly as they dared, harsh voices yelling: "Lowrey! Lowrey! Are you O.K?"

Manos was behind them, carefully picking his way down the slope, his cast like a monstrous cocoon on his chest. He was speaking to them, but no one was listening.

Then I remembered Cleo. I immediately swam back towards the spoon-shaped cove where she would have landed. There was nothing at the surface. I was pushing frantically through the water when I collided with something. Cleo surfaced a forearm's length from my face and laughed at my trauma. She had been hiding, it seemed. Her nose was bloody, but she probably couldn't taste it from the salt water. Her skin was splotched with the impact of the jump. Her brown eyes were bloodshot.

"You good?" I asked, in the only English I could put together fast.

"Amazing!"

Before I could translate another thought, she collided her face with mine, blue lips smacking the bottom of my nose.

"I feel super, SUPER!" she hollered, pushing off towards the others.

I let out a whoop and followed her ferociously kicking ankles. A few times, the miniature bloom of the fireworks rose above the ruptured water.

"Lowrey, you're mad!" the orange-haired wart said, as Stavros pulled Cleo out of the water. I hardly noticed that he put his hand out for me until I was being pulled up safely over the spines of purple sea urchins. Manos moved in to congratulate me.

"Not bad, *Erotiari*. Coulda landed a little smoother, though."

"Do a bomber dive next!" Andreas interrupted.

"You first, avocado."

With unspoken consensus, we all walked towards the seaside highway that led back to the motels. My headache and bleak thoughts had been forgotten in a dizzy euphoria.

While we were following the curves of the dusty road, Stavros pulled back to pace me.

"Aleko, I'm not your father, but you have to know what you did was very stupid. I've been diving for years. It's not something you do on a whim."

"Stavro *mou*," Manos interrupted, "Aleko is the best diver at the Philothei Academy."

"Ellas is a free country, Stavro *mou*," Andreas added, getting an elbow in the throat for his loyalty.

"Mano, you don't look like you've scored too high on personal safety yourself. Listen Aleko, I'd be happy to teach you to dive sometime on the smaller rocks. You're lucky you didn't bash your head. I hate to be an iron fist, but if I see you up there again, I'm gonna make sure your parents know."

"Go stick it in a fire," Manos muttered. Stavros had already moved ahead to talk to the women in his bartender's English.

I wasn't interested in what either of them had to say. I was composing what I would say to Cleo next when Mrs. Donakopoulos ambushed us. She barricaded the way and started to blow her bagpipe about how long we took with Andreas. She had apparently been up to the store long ago to check on us. Our only respite was when she shook and slapped her son.

The *touristes* gave sympathetic and amused glances, but kept walking. Cleo waved at me, turning down the path to the northern beach before I could respond. I guess they had already seen the Temple of Poseidon, because I never saw her again.

Andreas started to cry so that he wouldn't have to explain himself. Manos, a great man under pressure, told Andreas's mom that we had walked to the ferry port to have ice cream. Although this was the safest excuse he could conjure, we had to listen to accounts of children being crushed by foreigners on mopeds. Then there was our inconsideration about the time.

When we were finally given a chance to beat it, I realized I was late for dinner. My mother would surely have come down to the pool to fetch me. Manos and I decided that we would do best to split at the entrance of our complex.

As we hurried through the dry evening wind, I discovered that I was actually relieved to be parted from the women. One success was stressful enough, and I hadn't really wanted to test my advantage by expecting to be able to buy them *lemonathes*. With a sudden shudder, I recalled that I didn't even have any money.

"Tell me, did you grope her under the water? Did you kiss her with your tongue, you dirty monk?"

"You'd like to know!"

I didn't want to share my giddy chaos with Manos. It was something I planned to explore carefully that night, like a traveller in a foreign country, with all of the possibilities and scenarios yet to be experienced.

"If it weren't for that *malaka*'s rotted-out roof, it would have been me doing the groping. You'd still be standing up there like a drop-jawed nutcracker."

I decided not to remind him about the ice creams just then. Maybe he was afraid that his natural advantage was ending. I thought about this as I climbed the stairs to my apartment, where I was counting on the presence of my visiting aunt to cushion me from my mom's *megali fasaria*.

TESS FRAGOULIS

EXCERPT FROM

Hipster, Hit the Road

You are a young woman in full blossom, a Smyrnean rose with a scent as fresh and intoxicating as an orchard at sunset, and it is your father's task to find the appropriate man to pick you. Though your father is worldly and refined, and has travelled to the great cities of Europe and Asia, he refuses to let you do the picking with your eyes, ears and heart. This is out of the question, though it is you who will have to look at your husband's face until the moment of death, smell his breath on your pillow, feel the texture of his flesh as he lies with his full weight on your breast. These are not discussions your father will tolerate, and your spinster aunt is no ally. Neither understands that your dreams extend far beyond Smyrna and even beyond the City, where most of the primped up boys from good families come from. You picture your father in their fancy homes, raising a crystal wine goblet in celebration of the perfect match. The high notes born of their clinking glasses echo in your ears as if someone were thinking of you; but it is you who thinks of them as they implicate you without your consent.

Your dreams are filled with faraway places with foreign names, which you practice pronouncing until they roll off your tongue like a favourite song. Paris, London, New York: great cities you learned about when you attended the American College for Girls, and where some of your former schoolmates came from and went back to when their fathers' business in Smyrna was done. You have received letters from some of these young women and commit to memory every detail, every word they offer. It is your father's own fault that your head is filled with so much foreignness.

He was the one who insisted that you attend classes with the daughters of dignitaries, officials and rich men. But even without the privileged schooling, you still would not be interested in the tailor-made swells from Constantinople, their cheeks pink and smooth, their hair slicked back like Valentino's.

Your aunt despairs as you spurn each of these suitors, sending them away empty-handed, destitute. You reject them because of their looks, their age, their lack of wit, or whatever small imperfection you detect, which you blow up into monstrous proportions, large enough for even your father to notice. "What are you waiting for?" your aunt cries, tearing out her hair, pulling yours. "Do you want to end up like me, a spinster with no means?" You study her as she stands before you, exasperated, emaciated in the long black skirts she has worn since your mother passed away, and a *frisson* of fear spreads through your body, makes you wrap your arms around yourself. No, no, you do not want to end up like her, heaven forbid, in perpetual mourning for her lost youth, as dry as a tree that gets no sun or water and whose desiccated fruits will never be eaten.

You are waiting for the American naval officer you have christened Lieutenant Lovegrove to appear at your door, the gold buttons of his uniform bright as miniature suns dazzling everyone in their path. One afternoon in the front garden of a café by the water, as you sipped English tea out of a porcelain cup, you fell under the gaze of the miniature suns. You lifted the teacup towards your mouth and pretended to be absorbed in the French novel you had brought along—something by a woman named Colette. When the waiter delivered a note requesting the pleasure of your company on a walk along the Quais after the sun went down, you glanced at the officer and gave him a half smile, folded the note into your book, and walked out of the garden without looking back. You do not know how men and women conduct their affairs in America, but here in Smyrna, in 1922, young women from respected families do not accept invitations from strangers—not even handsome ones wearing impressive uniforms whom they have smiled at brazenly, and in whose personal sunshine they have basked. It is just not done, no matter what the travellers say. You keep his note as a souvenir, as proof of your power as a woman, and on the nights you sleep with it under your pillow you dream that Lieutenant Lovegrove is at the wheel of a black shiny car which drives you over the sea all the way to America. There you see, hear and taste the things your friends write about in their letters. You wear pajamas made of cat's fur, drink water that makes you giggle, and bite your handsome new husband on the neck.

These fancies bury every young man who comes calling, no matter how handsome, witty or rich. In any case, you are in no rush to get married, since you have learned from the foreign books you favour that anticipation is always more interesting than what is attained. You confide these thoughts to only one person, your cousin Amalia, to whom you write in a coded language the two of you have devised to hide your secrets from your parents. You feed her dreams with your imagination, your desires arouse hers, and together you create a fantasy world that cannot be penetrated by conventional proposals.

This afternoon your father is returning from his latest trip to the City. He will bring home presents, letters from Amalia, and his latest protégé. The house has been prepared to receive the master and his guest. Even before the young man is introduced to you, he will be seduced by the quiet luxury of the entrance way and parlour where he awaits your arrival; by the tastefulness of the silk kilims hung on the walls; the detail of the needlepoint tableaus; the artistry of the tessellated bowls and vases with their opaque glazes—magical vessels spread casually throughout the rooms. Yours is a house filled with treasures. You are so accustomed to their presence it is hard to imagine the impression they make on a stranger. But these decorations are just accessories to what the young man truly desires. You carry a hefty dowry made up of fertile land and satchels of gold coins. Your father, the silk merchant, has done well for himself. Your hand-picked suitor cares little for the lace table cloths and curtains, the linen sheets, the crocheted bedspreads and doilies, or the white silk peignoir wrapped carefully in thin white paper, lying at the top of your hope chest and waiting for your wedding night to make its debut. If he could see you in the nightgown, swaying in front of your mirror, he would give up all the gold in Anatolia for one kiss. When you think of marriage, you think only of beauty—the groom's, the bed's with its lacy skirts, your reflection in the mirror, in the discs of your husband's eyes, locked on you as you step into the candlelit bedroom in your virginal sheath.

Though you are determined to reject the man no matter what he has to offer, you play along. You choose a colourful dress that is both elegant and alluring, twist your hair back into a loose chignon held into place by a Castillian comb, letting a few capricious strands fall over your forehead. You slip on your finest shoes, the soft white leather ones reserved for holidays and weddings. And you powder your breasts with a fine talc that smells of exotic flowers which only bloom at night in the desert.

The young man, wearing his best suit and smelling faintly of lemon verbena, is enchanted as you step into the parlour holding a silver tray. You offer him tea and a sweet—a pink, sinful rose pastry that melts with the taste of Smyrna, of you, in his mouth. Though he does not know it yet, he is glimpsing that which will never be his. You smile as you imagine him remembering this moment bittersweetly every time the woman he will eventually marry brings him his tea. But while he is yours, you dazzle him with your many charms. You sing love songs to him in French and Turkish, play minuets on the blonde piano from Mr. Kasanova's shop, recite epic poems in Greek. You ask many questions about his home, his family, his ambitions and coo enthusiastically to his replies, no matter how dull. You treat him like a sultan, and even your father, who has witnessed this performance many times, is encouraged, though your aunt throws you dirty glances when no one else is looking.

You hope beyond hope that your father will give up his search, and you intensify your own down at the Quais and in the lovely cafés filled with charming and dapper strangers, with beautifully dressed women sipping lemonade or coffee, playing cards and gossiping while their doll-like children are fussed over by nursemaids. You spy on the women, copying details from their dresses into a small notepad you carry so that your favourite seamstress will be able to drape you in the latest fashions from abroad. In this manner, you hope to blend in. When you are feeling bold your favourite game is to fool these elegant women into thinking you too are a visitor to Smyrna. You speak in musical French to the Americans, in crisp English to the French. This, you assume, makes you seem more sophisticated.

These trips to the Quais on your own or with your black cloud of an aunt take place when your father is away on business, buying and selling silks rich enough for an emperor. His regular departures give you a freedom not enjoyed by other Smyrnean girls of your class. You pity them as you sip your lemonade on the terrace of the Sporting Club, strands of your hair tickling your cheeks in the warm sea breeze. From this vantage point you are free to observe the traffic of handsome young men below, who stroll by alone or in groups, and are thinking seriously, you imagine, about stumbling upon you like a rare treasure of the east, an Anatolian pearl that they will be unable to resist, which they will have to possess.

It is impossible for you to go anywhere alone at night unless there is an emergency: the need to fetch a doctor from a nearby house or one of the *gendarmes* who patrol your street, tapping their clubs on the ground to reassure citizens and forewarn miscreants. In all quarters of the city, once the sun goes down, young women are shut behind the white lace curtains of fanciful, glassed-in balconies or are caged in like pretty birds by the breast-shaped iron bars of ground-floor windows, where they lean forward on tender elbows and provide passersby the opportunity to look but not touch.

During the day you are free to come and go as you please, and excuses for your frequent *sorties* are easy enough: you are going to buy a piece of lace at Giorgiadi's, to try on hats at Moutafi's, or to browse for furniture for your dowry at the Xenopoulos department store with its four floors of luxury on rue Franque. These are all perfectly respectable reasons for a young woman of means to be roaming the streets alone, and sometimes they are even true. Smyrna has so many exquisite shops abundant with all the finery of Europe and Asia that to keep up with the *nouveautés* would be a full time job. And who could blame you for stopping at the Café de Paris on the Quai for a refreshment after all that labour?

Going out in the evening, however, is a different affair. And though it is customary for young ladies to visit the homes of friends and relatives after supper *en famille*, there is no adequate excuse in the entire world for an unchaperoned foray into night. For someone who has never learned to deny herself anything she truly desires, this constitutes an emergency, and calls for desperate measures.

You will escape your cage after night has blanketed the city; after your aunt has locked the iron gate at the entrance with a key worthy of Bluebeard and has bid you good night (but never pleasant dreams); after you have kissed your little brother Constantine and put out his lamp; and after you have balled up your laundry and stuffed it under the bedclothes. You were careful not to be overly pleasant to your aunt at dinner so as not to arouse her suspicions, which are sharp, paranoid and easily provoked. She has never entered your room after the lights are out, not even when you were a little girl crying through a nightmare. But you would not put it past her to suddenly appear at the threshold tonight in her terrible black nightdress, her ash-grey hair hanging down to her ankles. The laundry under the bedclothes is not likely to fool her if she takes even two steps into the room holding the dimmest lamp. So you leave a note that says you have eloped with the old hunchback bookseller who walks the streets loaded down like a donkey, calling out passages from *Les Miserables*, *Secrets of the Parisians*, and from tear-jerking romance novels your girlfriends devour like sugar cookies. He has other books that interest you more. Books collected from foreigners of taste and culture, full of deep and unsettling passions you would otherwise never know existed.

The crisis your flight would cause your aunt, who is your guardian while your father is away, is worth the punishment that will follow when you return long before the news reaches him in Constantinople. For she will spend the first few hours of your absence consulting neighbourhood women whom she's dragged out of bed, trying to come up with a plan of action to make herself look blameless. Next she will order a *gendarme* to track down and imprison the poor old bookseller. And only then will she notify your father, as full of anger as remorse. If the lights are ablaze upon your return, the iron gate ajar, you might just keep going. Why not? You can teach piano and singing in Rome or Paris, and go to l'Opéra whenever you please. You'll send your brother picture postcards from your travels with exotic stamps for his collection—this way your father will know that you are alive and well. You may even try to find that woman Colette, to tell her all about Smyrna and your great escape so she can write about you in one of her books. How could you help but become the toast of Paris society then? Such plans, such possibilities!

These are the thoughts spinning their drunken webs in your brain as you put on your blue hat with the discreet little plums, open the door that leads to the back stairs—the emergency exit—and come out in the garden. Like a burglar you stick close to the walls so as not to be spotted by your aunt or your closest neighbour, a widowed teacher with a permanent case of insomnia who spends long nights at her window staring wistfully at the stars. The streets are not as dark as you'd hoped, for a full moon flushes out all but the darkest nooks (must there always be a full moon over Smyrna on nights such as this?). You squint up at it from under your brim and tell it to turn its face from you, promise that you will be home soon, but it is implacable. It shines on you alone, following you through the streets, announcing your entrance into a life of secrets and vice for anyone who is watching.

Your eyes cast down, your beaded purse clutched to your breast, you shuffle past breathing doorways, growling dogs and mating cats until you reach the Armenian quarter, where no one knows you and where he awaits you under a lamppost. He stands casually, comfortably, inviting passersby to admire him in his uniform. The gold buttons lining his chest are as dazzling in the moonlight, under the glow of the gas lamp, as they were in the afternoon sun the first time they shined upon you at the café by the water. You watch him from a distance before making your presence known. He smiles when he sees you, tips his hat and offers his arm. You take it, smile nervously, and try to stop yourself from giggling, though the situation suddenly seems immensely funny. Unable to contain your laughter, it escapes into the night sky and echoes through the quiet Armenian streets like the ghost of a mad clown. Perplexed, he asks if anything is wrong, and you blush and apologize for your lack of manners. But the laughter has transported you from the recent past (your getaway) into the immediate future (the cinema) where your escort places his hand on top of yours while black and white images flicker across your face and music from the orchestra floods your ears.

It would be a lie to say that the light though insistent grip of the young officer completely distracted you from the film: Julio's tango in a smoke-filled cantina has impressed itself permanently onto your memory, and you vow to learn the steps before the next ball. But nor was there a moment while you watched that you were unaware of his touch. Even through your gloves you could feel the warmth of his skin, the blood pulsing beneath it. During the scenes where Julio kissed Marguerite, your upper lip quivered ever so slightly, but you glued your eyes to the screen, not daring to look towards your escort for fear you would become undone.

After the film has ended you forgo a moonlit walk along the Quai (you are not yet that brazen), but linger under a lamppost, listening and smiling as the officer speaks about himself and his home and the first time he saw you. You promise to meet him again without indicating exactly when or how this might be arranged. He does not kiss you goodnight, but watches you trot down the boulevard as the town clock strikes twelve, your hand holding your blue hat in place. You turn one last time to wave, and blow him a kiss before disappearing into the twisted side streets that will bring you to the back gate of your garden, where palm fronds and gardenias sleep and an unknown fate awaits you, fist to hip. (When you arrive, breathless and anxious, and find the house dark and unperturbed by your absence, you are more than slightly disappointed.)

Your wish to see the young officer again is as strong as your desire to commit him to your imagination where you can do with him as you please. Dress him up in costumes from the movies (a sheik, a cowboy, the king of the jungle), or undress him slowly, one gold button at a time until you can lay a naked hand on the warm flesh beneath.

You do see the officer again but in the company of your aunt, who becomes prickly when he nods to you in greeting and your pale complexion turns pink as a May rosebud. She demands to know why you are familiar to foreigners, since in her mind to be recognized is to already be compromised. You remind her that you attend all the important balls with your father, and ask her if she thinks you spend your time there dancing with a broom. You hope your insolence masks your guilt, and though she is a shrewd opponent, she cannot confirm anything, nor can she imagine that which she has never known. This is her one disadvantage. She did not grow up in Smyrna, but in a neighbouring village where the matchmakers' best efforts failed to accommodate her. Too skinny they said. If she ever dreamt of love, you decide, she forgot about it by morning. Though you have no immediate plans for another great escape, that night you slip the note about the bookseller under your aunt's door, then go to your room and lock yourself in. From under the bedclothes you laugh when you hear her shriek then trip up the stairs. She rattles the crystal doorknob and bangs her fists raw upon the solid wood door, which you do not open until morning.

The next rendezvous with the officer is aborted because of the sudden return of your father and yet another prospective son-in-law (you have concluded that your father picks these men more for himself than for you, like silk lingerie chosen by a French lover). You are not as impetuous with your father in command, but you can barely disguise your indifference to this latest prospect, not even bothering to play the charming hostess, feigning dizziness shortly after his arrival and retiring to your room until he leaves. But these visits are not a complete waste of time. It is here that you learn the basics of arousing desire, and that indifference is often a more potent tonic than charm. You send the suitors away without any hope, yet hope they do, whereas the officer, who you may or may not love, waits for you under the gaslight, wringing his hands instead of holding yours, and practising his proposal, not of marriage but of something more pressing and delicious. Perhaps these are just your secrets, your female fantasies while you are trapped behind the white lace curtains of the second floor balcony, and men do not have such ideas. You will not find out, at least not from that officer, who you never see again except when you close your eyes.

She was discovered, asleep (*under a piece of red cloth*), in a velvet-lined box of the Piraeus opera house. Others had been fetched by relatives or boarded in the homes of sympathetic strangers wearing black. This was different. Kivelli's benefactress was dressed like high queen of the gypsies: shiny red dress a few sizes too small for her mass, oversized purple hat with a golden plume.

"I'm Kyria Effie. Take your things," she commanded, neither kind nor mean, but matter of fact. "I have a place for you in my house." Things, there were no things. No questions. Kivelli put on her shoes and followed her down the stairs. Kyria Effie talked, talked, talked the whole time; it did not matter to her one bit that her charge was saying nothing. She wasn't looking for conversation, but for an echo to direct her out of the underworld. No Greek had been spared, untouched by the Catastrophe, not even this huge woman in her carnival outfit. She filled the world with words, noise; Kivelli shut everything (*dead bodies burning, smell of flesh cooking*) out. On the streets she shielded her eyes from the sun, the sights, mute and deaf to Kyria Effie's babble. When they stopped in front of a cracked, red door, a pain spread through Kivelli's chest and stole her breath. Perhaps she should have listened. Maybe run. But where? Back to the opera? No. Back to the sea.

They trudged up the stairs to a room no bigger than a broom closet. Windowless and dank, it had a thin mattress covered in rags on the floor, and a plain wooden chair in the corner. No better than the opera house, possibly worse, though it did have a door. Kyria Effie stood in the hallway—she wouldn't fit inside the room and didn't try. "This is your home now, my dear, and you can call me mother. All the girls do." Kivelli stared at her feet, at her broken shoes, too small and ugly brown. "You will be fed and clothed and given an allowance if you follow the rules."

It boiled down to taking it with her mouth shut. Except when required to keep it open. Kivelli was no stranger to "it." In the opera house, "it" was traded for an extra hunk of black bread, a second piece of herring. You took it, you gave it and were lucky to do so. But not Kivelli. She looked into Kyria Effie's wrinkled, painted face for the first time. Regurgitated words stuck like fishbones in her throat. "I will never call you mother. Do you understand?"

Kyria Effie grunted in reply, grabbed her by the arm, and dragged her downstairs again. She drew back a heavy curtain the colour of moss that closed off a dimly-lit room. Half a dozen old men sat on a threadbare sofa and on the floor, talking, passing a narghile between them. The one cranking the *laterna* stopped, and the mermaid decorating its top-board winked at Kivelli, who collapsed like a doll made of wood and string. "Please don't let any of those rotting louses touch me, buy me for a few coins," she begged, streaking Kyria Effie's polished shoes with tears, saliva.

Kyria Effie smirked, immune to such pleas: "It is the ones who don't cry that I worry about most, my girl," and pushed Kivelli through the curtain with her foot. She lay prone before the men, a woven carpet waiting to be unfurled and trod upon.

"Gentlemen, I give you the Anatolian pearl," Kyria Effie announced, glowing, proud. Kivelli peeked at her audience from under her arm. One of the tougher looking guys shook his head, pulled the end of his moustache.

"Heartless woman, I can still smell smoke in her hair."

"You just don't have the money, Manolaki."

The others laughed, like caught thieves.

Saved for the moment, she went back up to the broom closet and crawled into bed. Her sleep was like death—without breath, without dreams.

Kyria Effie was not as impatient as she let on (every profession has its own demeanor—the gravedigger is eternally sad, the madame greedy, pitiless.) In the morning she told Kivelli that the Anatolian pearl would not be plucked by some fumbling diver right away. She would be saved for a big spender who collected such rarities and was willing to pay the price. Until he turned up, Kivelli would help around the house and clean the rooms after her other "daughters" were done. Not after every customer, but after every five or so when a mustiness rose off the sheets and filled the room with a fug so thick that it blinded and suffocated with its intensity. Kyria Effie assumed this would help Kivelli become accustomed to the atmosphere, to the parade of men with their flies undone.

As the other girls lead customers to their rooms, Kivelli hid in dark corners of the hallway. She was not ashamed, nor did she consider herself superior to the girls whose rooms she cleaned.

They were poor souls like her, selling what they had to survive. Nonetheless, she did not want to be seen, known within those walls. What if someone from home recognized her in her wretchedness? Not a young man, some seller of pumpkin seeds she'd flirted with then spurned—those boys were all dead. But some lost old man, a friend of her father's who'd come to their house for dinner or lunch, carrying boxes of gold-wrapped Swiss chocolates for Constantine and her.

These were pointless fears. There was no one of importance left to tell.

When the moans and the creaking of bedsprings subsided, she slipped behind the opening door. In the empty room, she held her breath, felt her way towards the window fumed by stale cries of passion. Flinging open the wooden shutters, she let out a sigh that turned into a song: "*Kiss me on the mouth, I cannot wait...* " Despite her. To spite her.

Kyria Effie galloped up the stairs, graceful as a pregnant camel, her breath as offensive. "Make yourself presentable," she spat, "and then come to the parlour." Kivelli stared at her for only a second, frozen. "Immediately!"

She was not prepared for this moment. Though she'd been expecting it since she'd arrived. How many more weeks could she have gotten away with dusting battered headboards and shaking out dirty sheets? Kivelli went through the motions, powdering her face, rouging her cheeks, her lips in the hallway mirror. She ran her fingers through her short, black hair, and tried not to look herself in the eye. Then she walked down the stairs—as slowly as possible. Everything would be lost when she reached the bottom.

In the dusty parlour sat a short, fat man in a suit, mopping his brow and the underside of his chin with a white lace handkerchief that looked like it belonged to a woman. Was it hot in the room? Kivelli was shivering with cold and covered her mouth with her hand to keep her teeth from chattering. The man stood up when she entered, stuffed the handkerchief in his pocket, and took a step towards her. She stepped back, looked away. "Barba Yannis, this is Kivelli." Kyria Effie's clammy hand grasped her elbow and pushed her forward.

"I own a small tavern not too far from here," Barba Yannis began, and cleared his throat. "I heard you singing out the window like a nightingale, Miss Kivelli."

Behind her hand a half-smile formed—so she'd caught the big spender with one of the flirty songs she used to tease her suitors (*tailor-made swells, cheeks pink and smooth*).

"I've lost my singer and thought you might stand in for a night or two."

Kivelli nodded. Consented. She wasn't sure to what.

They bartered in front of her. Kyria Effie made it sound like Kivelli had been reserved for that night a hundred years in advance. They settled on the standard fee, times three, and he counted the money out into Kyria Effie's waiting hand. Neither asked Kivelli if she wanted to go. She was going to sing in Barba Yannis's tavern as surely as she would drop her drawers if that's what he demanded. Who was to say that wasn't part of the deal Kyria Effie had struck with him before Kivelli came downstairs?

She followed him out of the house as if there was a rope tied around her neck: silent, obedient, reluctant. Every few seconds, she looked over her shoulder. Girls squeezed into the gaudy hand-me-downs of dead women draped themselves over the ledges of the upper windows. They waved, applauded, blew kisses and spat—for encouragement, for luck, for protection against envy.

On the way to the tavern, Barba Yannis rattled off the names of a few songs. "Do you know any of them?" he asked hopefully.

A few sounded familiar. Groups of buddies full of hash and

good spirits sometimes brought records with them, sang along while they waited their turn and Kivelli served them drinks. Others brought instruments or sang unaccompanied, clapping hands, stamping feet for rhythm. They were rough songs—about jail and drugs and betrayal. Kivelli had learned a lot of things at Kyria Effie's.

"There aren't many women singers in Piraeus. Not like where you came from." Where had she come from? The opera? The broom closet? "But your voice lured me in like a lovesick fish, so I thought it might be worth a try." If it didn't work out, if the band or the men did not accept her, she still had her place a Kyria Effie's, Barba Yannis assured with a wink.

And the prospect of the Anatolian pearl finally being plucked.

cloth of worship

I

i am cut from the cloth of dangerous lovers,
of passion that stirs in the greek eye, longings for
far away ships, skies. i have waited
for jesus, walked the streets blind. i have
looked for you everywhere, by the river
with the old picnic signs. i have crawled under
tables, worshipped with spiders. you were
a sign and a crucifix—dangerous, dangerous.
i crossed the streets without looking, trying
to find you. i found a monastery, rang
at its door—delivered unto bells, saints...

II

don't come too close to my blind eye, i
still may see you and the sudden light of
your face. you, by the roadside, were
a gentleman. you stood beside me for hours,
wiping the rain from my face. it rained
for days, and still, i sat there, the horizon
moving. and you shone a light, those
fleeting moments in the ditch, me blind,
owing you something

III

your laugh is an infection i cannot prevent.
i blow you kisses, see them rise, strands of smoke.
i can hardly look at your shine streaming
through pores. you are a wish just before
the construction of glass

IV

worship in this mad hour of cross and flame. torn
wings and ancient photographs. i am a choreographer
of famous greek dances. i recall your longing for the muses,
your balanced laugh. you came one night as i was
hanging in the island air. i saw you twisting like a
holy robe. i worshipped you as risen light, amidst
five-pointed stars. you could've been a saviour,
your vision was the way

Oracle at Delphi

i keep writing about bones as if
i could pull something out of skin

over and over
to remember

curses
the eagle's stare

        in spurts

no one dares divulge
the cost
of vapours rising

i keep wondering when will my fingers
hurl me back

when will the Pythian voice reveal itself

        it is the wind that creeps
behind this tree
for certain   bones—

the stones are full of buzzing
—in this heat

Memory

inside the blood clots
the snow white is a figment, an illusion

                        statue—
at the centre of everything
snow sheltering

she can see the precise hand raised
the other, on extended knee

it's worship, this monument, this
frozen alabaster trick

still, she stops and listens to the ex-
cavated statue's outer shell

the face is immovable, the hand
that chiselled is long-gone

what is a memory?

in the midst of this invincibility
she unleashes flesh, blood at the centre
red heart across statue, snow

certain, there is something in the ice
that moves

Stavros Tsimicalis

Only from a child or a madman can you learn the truth.
—Greek proverb

I

Noon heat, and fear of frothing dogs, governs the empty streets.
An old man idles
In an irrigation ditch. He takes mud
And pitches it against
The white walls.

A few youngsters play on the riverbank.

One of them breaks away, draws a circle
Around himself with an oleander stick
And watches how the Nereid's dance.

II

He builds a labyrinth

Invites us to stroll and view
His creation.

Then departs, leaving us alone
To be amused, and wonder
At his architecture.

III

On the resurrection
He follows the orderly
Procession calmly, along with
The rest of the suppliants
With their white candles.
The only noticeable difference
That he carried a shovel.
His apology simple direct:
I came to bury Him.

The Last Time I Saw G.T.

At intermission
He was meandering
Through the crowd
In the waiting area

Without a lover or companion.
He seemed to
Waft above the crowd
And the people who
Were chatting
He seemed to be walking away.

Death caught up to him
On a street in Athens.

With a message in his pocket,
A hurriedly written poem
A few pomegranate seeds
And an old silver coin
Wrapped in silk.

◆

perhaps we should speak differently. the first steps
of a beginner. the sameness
of relics that constantly appear
in front of those that passed with certain
reverence.   blood, neglect of man, the grooved faces
of time under the sun.   singed face.   bright shield.
 fate is small. endless unfinishing is eros.
a shadow that does not grow. a light
that does not shrink. one line in the labyrinth.
a cypress tree on the other face
of death.   we have lost our nakedness.

◆

The autumn wind
Skims over your body
Like a soft hand

Unbuttoning your blouse.
No more words
No more whispers
Between the lovers.

Only the infinite
Desire to be silent
So nothing
Is betrayed.

Above us
A spider hovers
Motionless, suspended
Between two beams

An austere balance.

An immobile presence
Of eternity, rests
On a single thrust.

Mr. Frederick and Nancy Drew:
The Case of the Vacuum Cleaner Salesman

He sold more than we bargained for. As a salesman for my family's maintenance company, Mr. Frederick invested my father with the mechanics of a new idiom. My father discovered many words under his guidance, clever phrases gleaned during their drives to the office, at meetings with wealthy contractors. He became indiscriminately articulate. Our conversations at dinner turned into a surplus of polished sounds, words clattering like too much silverware: *specification, liability, proposal*. My father adopted a foreign affectation. He spoke with the immigrant's curious mixture of pride and humility.

"Where's Mom?" I yelled as I rushed in after school, dumping my knapsack of books on the kitchen floor. "*Specifically*, she is not at home."

"Is there a *proposal* you wishes to *disclose*?" he asked my unsuspecting friends.

"*Actuuually*, Irene cannot *dialogue* now. She is to *partake of victuals*."

Mr. Frederick sat beside him and beamed like a proud schoolteacher.

Or a missionary.

After dinner, he often delivered a dose of Bible stories. My brother and I stationed ourselves like sentries at opposite ends of the living room couch, with Mr. Frederick angled between us, spinning tales of sword-brandishing, avenging angels and sacrificial lambs from *The Children's Illustrated Bible*. I stared at the jeweled pendulum of his hand swinging right to left, left to right, as he turned one glossy page after another; the longer I looked, the more it seemed that the glinting sapphire on his ring finger held strange powers. Mr. Frederick was a man of brown polyester suits, bow-ties, and fedoras. His heady mix of mothballs and Old Spice smacked me with such insistence that I continually reeled back, and could never properly make out the changing images spread open on his lap.

The thud of the bedroom door signaled my entry into a world of my own. Mr. Frederick's Bible Hours lay on the other side of the domestic divide, and as I made my way to the Formica-paneled bookcase that ran the length of one wall, I imagined myself a sleuth: an oval-eyed, brown-haired Nancy Drew, in search of a story without borders.

Homer's *Iliad* gave way to *Alice in Wonderland* in my quest. When I scoured Herodotus's *Histories* for a glimpse of Helen of Troy, I discovered her whisked to the desert plains of Egypt, recounting the injuries of gods who had turned her beauty into a war cry. It was Euripides who finally reclaimed her virtue, and in reconciling her with the conquering Menelaus, generated my faith in heroes and romance.

"*The story is not true. You never went away in the benched ships. You never reached the citadel of Troy,*" Stesichorus said. And I learned that his curse of blindness was not so much an absence of light as it was a lack of alternate perspectives. After Stesichorus gave Helen the benefit of the doubt, he gained entry into a fathomless wisdom.

In my eleven-year-old mind, God lived in the slipstream between two points of view. His white room in the sky had two windows, one perpendicular to the other, just like my own. This was how gusts of air pressed through the secrecy of curtains. Rushing in through the open window to my left, airborne sounds from neighboring lawns climbed in diffuse bands towards the ceiling fan where they were caught by the radiating frenzy of blades only to swoop out the other window with its view of the schoolyard. Rainbows of breath suspended high above the animation of swings and the spray of the water fountain.

Like the clandestine operations of priests during the Ottoman occupation of Greece, who turned churches into schoolhouses so as to maintain their own alphabet, my studies involved a tilt of the head. Eyes flitting from one side to the other. An intake of breath.

Under Mr. Frederick's tutelage, my father became a hybrid creature, a Cretan Minotaur tamed by Canadian winters. When in anger, or in unfamiliar surroundings, he adopted a steadfast formality. The multiple patterns of his diction held together like a mismatched suit, snug-fitting and buttoned to the collar. His words became velvet place-settings in English parlors, and he would curl his pinky while sipping from porcelain teacups. Only with his Greek friends, playing backgammon or watching *The New Horizons* on TV, did he relax to a current of unrestrained sounds, the faint rumblings of wheels on gravel, olive branches bristling in the wind.

The day of *My Sentencing*, I detected a new strain of vocabulary. The moment I entered the living room, I was in arctic territory.

"Irene, take a seat. We needs to dialogue now," my father said.

"Irene, your father and I have held discourse on your extra-curricular reading. I have advised him some of your subject matter is highly objectionable," Mr. Frederick explained.

"What do you mean?" I set the tray of Greek coffee on the table, and quickly assessed the situation. On the floor by my father's feet sat two columns of books that earlier had lined my shelf: one stack held all my Nancy Drew Mysteries, and in the other *The Collected Tales of Edgar Allan Poe, Charlotte's Web,*

Gulliver's Travels, and a blur of other titles I couldn't make out from where I was standing.

"A young girl must be careful not to enter mind-altering intrigue," Mr. Frederick continued. "Especially a girl with your imagination, Irene."

"Yes, Irene. Mr. Frederick has gave it to my attention that this kinds of books is . . . is like drugs. They will make you filled with villainy," my father proclaimed, darting a glance at Mr. Frederick before wagging a finger at me. He paced about the room in the Blue Jays sweatshirt my brother and I had bought for him one Christmas, the starched collar of a dress shirt visible beneath the neckline. Even at his most leisurely, he maintained his guard on appearances, wore socks with his sandals.

My father picked up *The Quest of the Missing Map* from the pile. Carson Drew would never prevent his daughter from doing as she pleased.

"*You're a peach, Father. You let me do anything I like*," Nancy would chime, then blow kisses as she grabbed the keys to her blue Mustang and dashed off to expose the underworld of criminals.

"Dad, these are adventures. All my friends read them."

"Verily I tell you. From this day forward, I forbid you to read Nancy Drew."

"You can't tell me what to read!"

"I am your father!"

"Give it to me!" I cried, lunging forward. My senses rushed past me as if dismissed, and I wound up breathless but spinning. Before realizing what I had dared to do, I tore the mystery from my father's hands.

It floundered for a half-second before striking the floor, a robin or a fledgling sparrow, shorn of its feathers.

"Mom. Mo......mmmmmm. Come in here!"

"The whir of the blender erupted from the kitchen. I hoped it heralded my mother's sharp knife. And a big spoon.

"These books are outlawed from my home. You bring another mystery here, and I will burn it," my father stomped, knocking his shin against the mahogany coffee table.

My mother's best crystal vase toppled and rolled over the edge, a mess of dried roses littering the floor, a thorny carpet between us.

"Burn it. Burn it! You can't burn my books!" I stamped back.

"I can! And I will! I will burn whole cities to save you!"

Mr. Frederick leaned forward from his spot on the wingback chair, shards of lamplight cutting his profile into angles, jig-saw pieces that refused assembly. He brought the cup of Greek coffee to his lips.

"What have you been telling him?"

"Nothing. He said nothing. I am your father."

"**You** are. And **He** isn't!" I yelled, and glared at Mr. Frederick.

"What have you been telling him? Tell him it isn't true," I demanded, rising to my feet.

"I said nothing. I only directed your father to the illustrations. Your father made up his own mind."

On the book covers, Nancy was one step away from Mr. Frederick's twister of damnation. Treading up a winding staircase while guttering candlelight engulfed her in shadows, she looked ready to slide down the banister and into the pit of Hades. Or running through the forest with a grandfather clock in her arms, she turned fugitive and fled from an army of fanged demons.

Not even her blue tweed jacket and knee-length skirt, or the respectable weave of her silk scarf, could redeem the daredevil branding her soul in the eyes of Mr. Frederick and my father. She would have to fend for herself.

"Dad, have you read them?" I ventured.

"What?"

"Have you read the mysteries? You can't judge a book you haven't read."

My father stood facing the window that opened onto our front yard; shafts of moonlight pierced through the blinds, casting a wavering, golden halo around his head. He seemed as if he was disappearing, more spirit than flesh. Crossing his hands behind his back, he stiffened. I saw the mechanics of a repeated journey in the grid of his calloused palms: retreat and return. His forehead leaned against the glass. I held my breath, waiting for his pronouncement.

It was a midsummer night, but a heavy wind thrust itself against the walls, seeping in through the cracked caulking. It reached across the wooden slats of the floor, pushing me further away from the exit. Barricading me inside the makeshift shelter of my father's misguided notions. I wondered how many other daughters were held captive in the gathering winter of living rooms just like ours.

"Your father knows enough of mysteries, Irene. Like I said, he's looked at the covers and made up his own mind."

"Take the pile on the left back to your bookshelf. The pile on the right I will deliver somewhere else," murmured my father, staring through the glass.

"*Father, why hast though forsaken me?*" I muttered under my breath, and heard my mother slam another cupboard as I picked up my orphaned books and marched out of the room.

I was dying for a mystery. Nancy Drew would never allow herself to suffer such injustice. No villainous vacuum cleaner salesman could turn her from an independent girl detective to an itinerant moth threatened by the suction of censorship. In *The Bungalow Mystery*, she was knocked unconscious by assailants, only to wake up and find that her wrists were about to be tied. She used the detective's trick of holding one's hands together while being roped in, slipping the bonds later. In another instance, she used barnacles to cut through the ropes and swim to safety. I didn't know how to swim, and had never seen barnacles on The Danforth, so I decided that holding my hands, as if in study or prayer, was a better way of slipping from the unfairness that bound me.

I thought of smuggling in copies from the school library and hiding them between the covers of a larger book, *The World Atlas*, or my copy of *The Makings of the Greek Warrior*. I imagined snatching puffs of the illicit text while huddled beneath a blanket at the foot of the driveway, or in a corner by the chimney on the roof. Like some Dickensian waif, I would escape parental scrutiny, with only the scarf of my breath around me, and the odd chirp of birds.

One Saturday evening I marched into the living room with a mystery bundled in between the mountain of clothes I had drawn from the hamper, and announced that I was doing the laundry. "Go ahead, dear," my mother murmured, and returned to her needlepoint. "But make sure to go through the pockets first."

My father was engrossed in the newspaper and didn't seem to be listening. I hadn't spoken to him for weeks, barely nodded when he passed the bread to me at dinner, or when he picked me up from school. But I thought it best to appear repentant. He had taken to peering into my room whenever I was studying, to make sure I wasn't led astray by *corrupting editions*. The laundry room seemed my last refuge. Either that, or open warfare. "Okay, Dad? I'm doing LOTS AND LOTS OF LAUNDRY," I yelled across the room, and hoped that I sounded convincing.

When I reached the basement, I thought I'd faint from relief.

I dipped a finger under the water-flow of the washing machine, and made a sign of the cross on my forehead.

Peeling back the soiled tangle of sleeves and pant-legs as if unwrapping a Christmas present, I loosed my hardcover mystery from its bindings, and carried it towards the light. I placed it on the shelf by the box of detergent and bleach, and began sorting the laundry into two piles.

The laundry room also served as my father's utility closet, industrial-sized vacuum cleaners of various makes like pot-bellied guards cramping every available walkway. Long hoses with ribbed skins and brush-wire heads snaked across the black and white tiles before disappearing into the narrow passage between the furnace and water boiler. The smell of engine oil invaded the room, the fumes making me dizzy.

I felt like a pickpocket as I fumbled through fabric looking for mislaid coins and bills. Taking that long-anticipated drag of outlawed text didn't seem like a good idea any more. Most nights when I followed Nancy up to the guttering light of the staircase, ambushed by the twin tricksters of dread and suspense, I stifled the urge to shoot under the bedcovers and abandon her mid-scene. Tonight I considered making a run for it.

But in the end, it wasn't my fear that undid me; it was a slip of paper with my father's signature on it. The moment I laid my eyes on it, I passed through the revolving door of my senses, and into the void of the unexpected. The walls of the laundry room withdrew, leaving only the pot-bellied guards of vacuum cleaners in circles all around me. My ears filled with the drone of spinning motors and I was pulled backwards, dragged across the black and white tiles as if sucked by an invisible hose. The brush-heads gathered momentum, repeatedly changing directions, and as I tried to staunch their wrath with what lay in front of me, a bunched towel, my bare hands, the slip of paper, they yanked the ground from under my feet and knocked me to the floor: I was whisked into the vacuum of the untold.

"Father," I cried out. "Where am I?"

A crowd of strangers blocked him from my view. I was in a desert of traveling souls. Men of all nations and manners were sweating under the burden of hardware essentials. Some carried boxes full of hammers, others supplies of wood or brick; all had tools for trade. All wore Mr. Frederick's brown polyester suits. Women in long skirts carried parcels of children. Up ahead, a waving banner in the sky relayed an impossible hope: *The New World.*

My father, towing a wagon of sealed boxes, stared straight ahead and walked alone. His ribboning breath conveyed him, and he moved forward. Not even in pictures had I seen him this young. He was barefooted in his sandals. Every few steps, another box disappeared into the desert's hollows, stirring up dust as he lightened his load. He stopped often to wipe his forehead. I pressed through his trail of losses, until I reached him at the border.

The sky darkened instantly, evacuating daylight as if it had pulled a drawstring.

All around me, people prepared for departure. I heard wailing goodbyes, the claps of the hurried embraces that allow one body to declare itself to another, despite the interrupting distance. Despite everything.

My father was sorting through his only remaining box. He drew a weather-beaten book from its depths, and cradled it in his hands. Lifting it up and down, up and down, as if to inscribe its weight in memory. Turning the pages of a story that could not survive translation. His native words for bread, water, love. His first signature.

In the instant it took for him to tear the pages from their binding, I saw the greatest sacrifice: a desert furrowed with every parent's small privations, countless ministrations. A network of unacknowledged carpenters raising households from the first floor to the last. How a vacuum can in time become a doorway. The mechanics of a vision. Outstaring the distance, I praised the hidden miracles.

When I found myself standing in the middle of our living room, I held a barnacle in my hands.

"Mom," I panted. I couldn't stop blinking. My eyes stung with the afterimage of a name.

I looked at my father reading the newspaper in his sandals and socked feet; the cross-stitched sheets of fabric strewn across my mother's knees. At the wingback chair in its spot in the corner by the window. And suddenly I knew it would take years for me to find the beginning, the place to be in. We are our secrets.

"Mo......mmmmmm. I'm going to take a bath. A long, very long bath," I said.

"Go ahead, dear," my mother murmured, returning to her needlepoint.

"Oh, and by the way dear," I heard her say, when I was halfway out the door.

"The next time you go down to the basement, hold on to the slip of paper. It's your only passport through the borders."

My mother's words have carried me further than I ever expected. Slips of paper are still my passports to discovery. I was born in a city of migrating hands; my stories are a collective ambition. Like Nancy Drew, I am ghost-written. Mr. Frederick went out west in search of other missions. I often imagine him as having hooked up with a band of plumbers, installing supernatural drainpipes in the homes of the disbelievers. My father still bursts into the room with his dialogues. But now I'm ready for the adventure.

MARGARET CHRISTAKOS

EXCERPTS FROM
Charisma

FROM "Cameo"
Often she finds butchers flirtatious; out on Danforth Avenue where the anemic lamb carcasses suspend for three or four seconds her trust in bodily safety, before the mind rescues her from moral crisis. Just a piece of meat like any. It's the hook, the hook that hooks, that perforates the eye, the brain, the guts of sympathy which must be let down, rinsed and laid in the cedar drawer until autumn. A time when ghouls are acceptable again and the skeletal dance of baby sheep is seasonally admired. Dressed in his white blood-smeared coat, he is like any irresistible and prodigious surgeon. He wears the coat, the lamb's clotted juices and pristine plate glass. He sees the world through hooked sides of things. Why be afraid?

Flirtation has to do with how the lambs are led along the corridor of doom. How they go and go. How they continue up the ramp while their cousins shriek. It has nothing to do with Easter. With men and beasts, rather, and strangers who may be beastly though their flirting may become on occasion beautiful. The natural frame of the plate glass composes him in savoury labour, up to the wristwatch in precision. He peeks through the space where the organs were to a woman's tenuous shock. Hooked by the blood of someone else. Thing else. Some other thing's public juice. And the fixed sway of the dead meat muscle—Cameo is a sitting duck.

Cameo coaxes the lamb chops from their wax paper sleeve and lays them on sizzling garlic. She scoops mint jelly into one of her mom's old teacups, and amuses herself while the meat goes bloody by holding the porcelain overhead—there they are, as delightful as when she was a girl, green shadows flickering through the cup's delicate filigree. Impatient to eat, she flips the chops, sniffing in their high corduroy bloom, flexing her knees to an old disco song. Gradually the element's blue flame singes her dreamy gaze and she fidgets with her too-tight bra strap, then jets her arms out at right angles and croons into the kitchen window, hopping from one foot to the other and pulsing her hips. Soon, the smell is so velvety she is near euphoric. She unloads the shining chops onto a plate, spoons coleslaw on top of the steaming jus puddle that runs off them, selects her favourite bone-handled cutlery, and sets these, a napkin and a beer on a silver tray. As she passes the hall mirror, she transfigures the carefree, dimpled smile on her face to a farcically enamelled grin, and, childlike, the round-jowled reflection catches itself awkwardly, averting its eyes, a dinner guest of inferior status. Well, fine. She just wants to fade in front of *The McNeil-Lehrer Report* while reading *Interview*. Clarence Thomas is deplorable and River Phoenix has siblings named Rain, Liberty and Summer, and Keanu Reeves is part Hawaiian—so that's it—explaining his preternatural gaze. She thinks about licking his eyelids. She doesn't mind such overlays, allowing that the real Keanu and his big-screen simulacra have little in common. The pastoral fogs up and loses its colour when she remembers Keanu went to the same high school as an ex-lover's sister, Korona, the mesmerically sirenic just-past-teenagehood dyke who moves like a rock stud at the Marzipan Room. Same eyes. She considers herself curled up in a wet tongue licking those eyelids. Then the newscaster misses a beat describing a murder-suicide in which the ex-boyfriend used two industrial meat hooks to set up the nooses. She shuffles into the kitchen, unloads pink bones into the garbage, rinses her plate and balances it in the dish rack. Humming an unforgettable TV ad promoting eternal brand loyalty, she flicks the one-cup switch on the espresso machine and reaches for pungent cinnamon and powdery, bittersweet cocoa.

On the phone they chat incessantly, like the cable universe, like a DEEE-LITE tune played on every radio station simultaneously. Cameo mentions how her course is progressing, everyone stalled in the personal again/ *oh brother*; the eerie overlap of the butcher winking at her during the pendant midpoint of the afternoon/ *that's strange*/ you're telling me; and then the story on the news that snagged even the commentator's speech/ *fuck, how horrible*/ men and rage, eh, women don't/ *do that*/ no, we just/ *hurt ourselves*/ yeah. She avoids mentioning the meat she had for dinner, finding her own choices often inexplicable, and besides, Mae is vegetarian this year. Without guile, Mae asks what *Interview* magazine is. *My Own Private Idaho* was so good I had to get it, says Cameo. Mae hasn't seen it. Cameo tells her about the film's two young gay hustlers, and how as the credits rolled she wished she too was a nineteen-year-old boy as flexile and free-floating as River. She doesn't say that she turned on to the thought of rubbing viripotent cocks with another equally accommodating gay boy, of mounting and fucking him up the ass enthusiastically. She can't brave such details unless Mae asks, and Mae stops short after chuckling agreement, then blurts, Look, Dustin's home, let's get together tomorrow for dinner, then we can really talk.

Cameo goes to the local butcher, a garrulous older Polish woman, because the baby needs lots of iron and protein. Hardcore nutrition. This meant meat and potatoes, meat and rice, meat and pasta when Cameo was growing up. Lamb stew, pot roast, liver and onions, spareribs with ketchup applied during the last ten minutes to get a braised country look. She imagines the placental tissue forming, a red sirloin in the epicentre of her psyche. Like drawings she happened upon at a gallery, of galactic uteri with trees and dreams growing inside. Already her own dreams make her anxious. She takes a baby boy home from a supermarket, and somehow he can already talk. She writhes about rubbing herself while holding him tucked under one arm, then says, Do you want to lick me? He wags his tongue, starts slurping at her vulva. After a moment he stops and looks up, cream all over his soft little chin. She runs the tapwater and says maternally, Do you want a drink? She tells people who ask that she's keeping him if no one claims him back. The dream's meaning escapes her over the cup of coffee she leans into the next morning, before she goes to the deli where the Polish butcher will wink at her, Ah, look at the glow on that one, making a big deal, and Cameo will like the invasive boastfulness of her, the European excess; her motherishness.

All week, in fact, she thinks a wordless blur of foodstuffs. The bakery woos, Fresh Valentine Cakes Available. Signs like this keep Cameo on track from day to day, remind her that English is the official language even for her meandering body's new require-ments. When the other butcher, the young one out on the Danforth, slicks his sweet right eyebrow to the ceiling, he is flirting in the queen's own tongue, though his first language is probably Greek. In a fit of *hysteria libidinosa* he might mutter in his mother tongue if she lapped his incurvate dimples. Or would he wish this? Cameo silently paraphrases in pig Latin how he undresses her in quick swipes, *opchay, opchay, opchay,* why waste such a precise and professional syntax! Try to make sense, baby-mother, she chides herself, tenting her shoulders forward to contain the cross-continental sound loop. A sign propped up in the cooler says, Fresh Lamb Whole Or Pieces Suit Your Fancy. Speechless again, she sees that the flirtatious butcher's open freezer is layered with the slight upside-down leftovers of lambs dreaming the disembodied envelopes of fur back onto their rib cages. She starts shivering. He says, What'll it be, miss? With those eyes, he could be her cousin. When Cameo comes here she dislikes the imbalance, like she's a plate in a dish rack about to topple, but she does come. And each time: the frightening image of a man with a knife imposes itself into the hem of her ahem-hawing as she stands at the pink-smeared counter. For what order to be uttered, or redress to arise. Sawdust in her nostrils, metal blade at her view's rim. Always at the edges his hand the wrist the blood the appetite. Sudden. Her eyes close.

One of the good ones: Cameo is waving a red scarf like a matador's cape. White rage pours out of a bull's snout. A green-clad crowd stamps in time, an overstuffed septic heart, glowing. She raises her perfect paws with one baby claw extended and says, No, take this. The scent of lavender wafts past each nostril. Then she is choking, flipping her forearms about until the sand shifts, and she coughs off a cloud of it. Mother woodchuck bleats an evening song, baby's favourite, Now you are whole, now you are one. When she wakes she sees the bull has gored her badly. Oh mama, let's get ice cream. Mama is paying the florist. Then it rains and pours and she is propped among cushions at the fireplace, her beige fur only tinged a little with red and she is trying to learn how to whistle.

In the sun, after some caffeine, time restores itself to a proper tick-tocking rhythm and Cameo recalls she needs new garments for her disappearing waistline. A chic recyclable paper bag full of freshly ground beans is stowed under her left elbow. As she shuffles through racks of large gingham dresses and broken-in denim overalls, waves of coffee aroma beguile the bored sales staff standing around and one by one they ask to break early. The manager comes over and scowls at her: No food in here allowed! Cameo hoots lightly, You can't call this food really. *I can.* Cameo pulls her eyes into the spaces next to her nose and snaps out a line from *thirtysomething*, It's time for you to find a therapist! The hunk Michael had reached the crest of yuppie success and could now explore alternative holistics. Cameo imagines the shrink— whom she quit seeing after he deduced she had *serious mother issues* (My mother died horribly when I was fourteen, go fuck yourself! she had said, slamming the last payment down on his side table)—she imagines this wing nut sitting across from Michael negotiating a sliding scale for the tremendously loaded. Ah, what if he could admit to the crush he'd so obviously repressed for his gay sidekick at the agency? Cameo weighs whether Michael screwing his work buddy would be as projectively sexy for her as River's *Idaho* scenes; nope, she decides, America's prime time infatuation with homosexual marginalia is always as compromised by disdain as it is hot. Who could tell really which had the upper hand, saucer-eyed imitation or the same old hateful wet dream leaking through the moneymongering cover of early evening, when unspeaking couples gaze deep into each other's emptiness through the quadrachromatic screen (the postmodern fiction she's reading leaves her feeling cyan). I was leaving anyway, this stuff's junk, she retorts. Don't waste my time! the manager yells after her, don't you know what time is? Oh yeah, scoffs Cameo, time is everything!

What Mae and Cameo need to talk about, admittedly, dates back a few months. Cameo says she'll order calzones from Dona's and toss together a salad. They drink soda water with lemon, for the baby's sake/ *a little sacrifice*/ worth it/ *you bet*. Just as their mood is getting productive, while Mae is casually setting the table, the phone rings. Cameo answers and falls immediately quiet. Listening from the kitchen counter, Mae whispers, *What's wrong?* Cameo mouths, My aunt. Mae grimaces. Cameo turns away and covers her ear. Okay, she says, whenever you can-really? All right then. Well—no, that's okay, I'm fine—fine—you know me—um hmm—bye bye. Bye. When she turns back, her cheeks look puffed, compliant. Mae says, Sweetie, you okay? Oh yeah. Yep. Yes yes. So should we order? Let's order.

It's really good/*it's great*/ good/*good*. Their two bodies reso-nate within softly metred conversation, two firm but conscien-tiously low timbres alternating, giving equal time, interin-flecting—so polite, Cameo ruminates, chewing on a wad of savoury mozzarella, nothing like my complicated wishes. The way Mae uses her fork like a pastry brush on the dinner plate, pushing bits of green pepper around in oil, skating excess onion over to one edge, those jittery strokes drive Cameo wiggers. Sorry I /*forgot*/ oh/*that's all right*/then. They've talked about their unique friendship, how all women do not necessarily mortar each other's sentences the way they do. No/*definitely*/ not/um/ hmm. The soft rolling of lips on consent, as if a favourite dessert. Cameo sets down two mugs of tea. I put the milk in/*okay*?/ okay. Mae smiles. Cameo grins back, swayed by a familiar arc of longing in her tongue's nerves to trace the gleaming tissue of Mae's bottom lip. Then suggests moving to the couch. *So do you want to talk about*/ yes/*I guess*/ I'm/*nervous*/nervy/*that makes two of us*/ which one?/ *both*. Grinning still, and fixed, like a card game. Unrevealing faces. Separate, folded hands.

Once Cameo had thought about mother's cream in a strange way, a way she could not after that first time continue to speak of. She began to live it in code, through images of food, since cream *was* a food to begin with. There was no other sort of cream she could allow out of a mother's body. When she thought of cream or milk her thoughts often turned quite pleasurably to snow, and then her arms would be swimming in it, folding it back onto itself like slow motion film images of milk spilling on a tabletop. Liking this picture, she had always wanted to go swinging in a snowstorm, but was thwarted by Parks & Rec's policy of packing the playground away in late November. Children were known to get overheated and absent-minded in their snowsuits, and the city could not be responsible for them burrowing sleepily into snowbanks and freezing to death. She had almost frozen once, surrendering too long on the walk home from school. The cold felt like milk being swallowed as it slowly entered her, and she thought of her mother, paying the babysitter for the hour of lunchtime she was wasting flatbacked on the bank, thinking of milk and a creaminess she couldn't place but missed somehow, like snow angels in summer.

Cleaning the apartment room by room, looking through old photographs, napping, Cameo passes days without seeing a soul. And then there Butch is, with his bloodied apron and the cartilaginous smirk she wants to mold between her thumbs. Instead, she leans toward the chicken trays and asks for boneless breast meat, if it's fresh, for a stir-fry. That's not the Greek way to cook a bird. Butch looks her full in the face and declares, You're Greek. Um, half, but I don't speak it. He clucks his tongue against his teeth. So it's all Greek to you, *capiche*, and then chuckles. Right, manages Cameo, thanks. Thank you, enjoy your meal, next time I'll teach you some Greek. Yeah, well, ciao for now, Cameo pauses, her feet stuck in the sawdust, and then her mouth moves around the words, my name's Cameo, Cameo Exstasias. Wow, says Butch, you're not kidding Greek, my name's Mike, but please, call me Mikopoulos for short, HA. The creamy whites of his brown eyes hold her in frame. Ever responsive to subtext, Cameo burps. Come back and tell me how dinner goes, instructs Mike. Finally Cameo hauls open the door and holds it there as the chimes attached to it unsettle and clamour and croak.

April sky's time-lapsed light, quick-shifting through blues and pinks and mauves, matches the folding over of phases in Cameo's belly. The firm mound of her uterus has softened, become unlocatable, like a hazy discomfort finally diagnosed only never to present itself again. Once, when her hands were small enough to be eclipsed by arrowroot biscuits, and her navel was the earth to her nipples' floating sun and moon, she sailed to sleep hugging her Raggedy Ann for a moonlit ship adventure. She leapt awake into unruddered darkness, screaming icily that Raggedy was mincing all her favourite pyjamas and scattering them in the sea. As an adult she has never matched the ferocity of that scream, can't even pitch the little flags of her panic-stricken palm-sweating or nervous cramps on the same wave-wracked map of experience. More often than not, when anxiety hits, her voice feels held under, pinched, easily disputed. The word her uterus speaks now is pregnant, you are a *pregnant* woman, you're tired because you're *pregnant*, and she mouths back, are you sure? I can't hear you, say it louder. She rubs her fingers into the gulley above her pelvic bone, playing doctor like when she was a kid, but feels the mush of spring thaw, feels sponge, feels the word empty. Running on empty, the way she's lived for so long, ever since her mother was killed.

Catastrophic, her mom's trip to the French River that weekend with Aunt Chloris. Chloris's plan, for her sister to, at long last, make peace with her hip therapy-savvy girlfriend over mint tea and trail mix, as if her mother needed this, has tormented Cameo into adulthood. At a stoplight, a hitchhiker leaping into the back seat of their car, requesting the vehicle for a joyride to Montreal, pulling a knife on them both. From the driver's seat, Chloris's half-delivered elbow chop to his breastplate and, flinching, him dunking the knife into her mother's left lung. She'd lost it, then, the grip she'd thought she'd have forever, and slipped away bloodily. Cameo didn't hear about it until the next day, when she capitulated to her still-true childishness, her need for home. It had rained unabatedly. Running away in defiance after her mother found out she was dating her high school math teacher had been rendered an empty card. She relinquished her draw, figuring her mother's enviable poker face would call the ante infinitely now. The fact that her mother hadn't even known of Cameo's intention to leave, and instead had cut out on her, was a bruising shock. For a while Cameo saw her aunt as a warped heroine, an inconsolably ruined portrait of helplessness whose colours faded out at the edges, the lover's image brutally ripped away, and then, for a few years after Cameo turned eighteen, as a self-serving monster, a hyena, a scourge. That first year of university she worked through most midnights into the witching hour, through tremours quaking her spine at four AM, deaf to her body's common sense. Shut up, she'd say, I've got work to do, you can sleep tomorrow. See, ta-da, pulled off another miracle, sleepyhead, told you: the body is just a wall to be gotten past, a corridor once you find it, leading directly to the brain's unreasonable but right sort of clicking. Cameo's theory was hard to wrest from the dark spaces beneath her eyes, hard to rub out of her tight shoulder. Just was, like a gene clot. A birthmark, like the raised brown one adjacent to her navel below which the baby was now saying I to its first roll call: *Pregnant*. And here she is, at half past ten PM, barely awake but held by the blood of this other mouth speaking under the new sway and dip of her bowels, missing the hard pear shape that she is used to squeezing nightly in her self-monitoring ritual after kneading the bell of each breast, checking the bulk of her hips, scolding her thighs' softness. Pillow talk. In its pregnant place is this shifting out-of-season unknown. This leftover listening she isn't good at, keeping her fast asleep at night beside herself.

Sometimes Cameo feels like the carcass slung on the silver crook, the freshly stripped and gutted one mounted in the showcase to attract discerning customers. When she stops to look *through* the plate glass she finds her own face grafted *on* the plate glass looking back at herself, soft into the desiring hook of her eye. Perhaps she is the woman she likes to flirt with, midday, as much as she flirts with her threshold for abjection. Yes, part of going out into the world each afternoon is to catch herself in it, raw and available. She slowly learns how to protect the butcher, who winks and waves from inside the shop, from her gut hankering for the woman between them.

From "Marilyn"

It had to be you, it had to be yoo-ou, Auntie Seal might have been singing. Cameo is just waking up, mewing like a scruffy kitten. Hello, sweetums, auntie says, lifting Cameo onto her chest and holding her soft and still for *plenty*. Plenty of comfort, what you deserve in this rotten world, she whispers in Cameo's ear, still scarlet and hot from pressing in the pillow, hot from dreaming about the swing set at the park, chinooks in general. I dream happy, Cameo enunciates to auntie. Oh you precious, marvellous, wonderful one, auntie croons. You fantastico. You blizzard of talent—*Really*? Cameo swims in her aunt's grinning. *I'm*—You are so so so so so sweet. You wrote the book. You are the tune's tune.

Happiness has to do with how the sleep goes and goes away, flood water evaporating into mist. Cameo's eyes brighten, she pushes upright and steps into the word *Hi*. Speaking first in her own person and then in the echo of her aunt's spritely eyes. Wanna come, sweetums, and meet Marilyn? Her aunt deftly snaps closed the hand pouches on Cameo's jumpsuit, wedges each cluster of toes into its rubber envelope. Let's go fast, auntie says. *Fast*, Cameo doubles, the way she doubles everything in her aunt's face, her sparkle, the discourse of her desire, Cameo would say now. *Discourse* and *desire*.

That night, the mother and the aunt sit on chairs pulled tight to the kitchen table. Their elbows grind into the wood surface connecting them. A glass of milk slides around in its own white spillage. Don't you ever take Cameo there again. How can you be so pigheaded? Don't you speak about me, we're talking about you. You have no right to talk about me like this, Chari, you have no clue. All I know—Is nothing, is pig shit. Is what is *moral*. Your morality is a castoff, from Dad, from the system, from the goddamned church. And what happened to you, how did you get to be so selfish? Being true to myself isn't selfish. No, Seal, what you are is confused, and I want you to keep my daughter out of your selfish confusion. This isn't Cameo's problem, it's yours, can't you admit it? If anyone here's got a problem, Seal, it's you, *end of conversation*.

Cameo backs down the hallway chewing the tough thumbnail she has detached absent-mindedly. Her mother's curt voice flip-flops like bad perfume in her senses. But Marilyn gave her two balloons. Aunt Chloris bought them all ice cream cones, and together they had swung her in giant leaping steps up the grassy hill. She had been dangling like a fish, giggling heartily, and the women both guffawed, A fish? You're a whale of a girl, and don't you forget it!

Women's creamy cream. Their *cream*. Mama's *creaminess*. Ooosshhh.

From "Cameo"

Midnight's doorstep barely lit by a quarter moon, an eternity of humid silence which waving through makes measurable. Cameo watches Mike's solid shape lope toward the streetcar stop, peers past saw blade streetlights at his pleasing silhouette ducking up a sidestreet instead. Senses a displaced cawing deep in her blood, almost like the sex being memorized into compact code, her mood murmuring toward some distant backroad or shore. She moves up her stairwell stripping off her dress and topples immediately back into the rumpled, slightly rank bed. Lights out. Dreams of new snow falling in the shape of angels, and the child sitting up on a beach shaking off granules of hot blue sand.

When she was a girl there was a set of swings in the playground which Cameo considered hers. If other kids used them she congratulated herself on her bigheartedness. Wind was a healing thing. The adventure of her body moving in space, hinged to gravity by two iron hooks scooped into rings, was worthy of a weekend's planning. During the week she dreamt of it. *Whoosh. Shhrr. Whoosh.* She wore a red velvet scarf that flapped behind her neck. In the dreams sometimes she also wore her new skates. In the bad version her body would turn into a saw, blood splashing out behind. Sunday afternoon swinging in the breeze grafted her body to wholeness again, and the health of her daring. She surrendered to the image until her stomach got queasy. Then she leapt off the wooden seat, twinning her feet to the prints she'd prepared in the muck below. Ee-i ee-i o, she yelled. There's a hole in my pocket, dear Liza, whoever you are. And, how now brown cow, at the quartermaster's sto-o-ore. She would skip home, humming, with all the wind in her.

Cameo did her growing near domesticated water and rock where her guilelessness about nature's volatility was never tested. In winter she thrust her bare hands into snow banks and pulled out frozen weeds, chewing on their crisp stems like an arctic explorer lost in the tundra. During their snowmobile outings, her father's face wore frost like powdered sugar, it suited him, made him softer. While he lit his cigar and ulcerated the afternoon sky with loon calls that ricocheted across the lake, Cameo would stare at the tiny crystals melting on his bemused forehead and eyelids. His mouth was always in motion, as if stillness, not silence, spelled danger. She grew used to having something bodily to watch, a precursor to always leaving the television on later when she got to university. This man had thin shoulders and parched skin, he had a deep bias against the slow waltz, and a crisp odour, like ice, even when he was overheated. Despite his natural reserve, he managed to soothe the horror out of every evening after Cameo's mother died, when Cameo, striving for complication and risk and unfettered impulse, would go berserk dancing in her room to The Clash instead of attending to any of her homework. He seemed to understand her panic, and eased it, by inviting her out for boat rides on the lake whenever he could, and giving her blasts of cold, uninterrupted wind. She would close her eyes and feel the breeze raise goosebumps on her arms. Would even start to sing a little as the boat zipped around the bay, chilling her to the bone, mosquitoes knocking against her forehead. Keep going, Dad, she would shout, one more turn! He could sit several feet away from her and feel effective; he could disperse his own loneliness into the wind that shunted from her body to his, two seats behind, where he clutched the motor handle, observed the sun sink. And let the wind blow them.

A year and three months after the murder, her father flew to the Aegean for a month's vacation. He kept his pledge to send Cameo a postcard every few days; in shivering script in the ninth note was the message, *Dearest Cameo, your heart won't like this, but mine is hurt just as if that knife had punctured me. Your mom would have wished me this spare happiness. I'm staying for another month with my new friend, Strina, and she will come home with me in April, after the lake opens. Tell Auntie Seal I will pay for the rent again. Stay strong, Dad.* Cameo stared at the postcard photo, white goats intervening on a country road, a Greek farmer looking up at clouds. In her makeshift bedroom at Chloris's, she pinned it to a small bulletin board alongside the other scenes, the turquoise seascapes, alabaster rubble, a three-legged donkey. On the ceiling over her chesterfield, she taped her own grinning fourth grade picture. The mother was not apparently present. But Cameo knew, in that era, in her innocence, she meandered to school chanting tunes sung originally by the woman, at the top of her voice, washing dishes after the late night news.

After submerging the blade in the woman's chest, and keenly aware of the driver braking the car to a halt, the bandit broke the seal of the car's back door and dove out onto the sidewalk, rolled with a groan, leapt to his feet and jackrabbited into a nearby sewer tunnel. Chloris recorded only the least helpful of details: the bottoms of his shoes were white rubber, his rear end was youthful in form, there had been dirt under the nails of the hand menacing the knife before she walloped him, upgrading his notoriety from two-bit megalomaniac to first-degree murderer on the run. She clutched her sister's neck, lifting the head so that their profiles were mirror images, both locked in sobs, both imploring the other's total attention. They stared into each other like this until the one died and the other fainted. When Chloris reawoke, she saw the world sideways from the curb up, and in the centre of her vision was the shape of her sister under a white sheet. She stood up and cried out her sister's name, *Charisma*, and then Marilyn's, and knew she'd become what people watch on the news before bedtime and scoff at, saying, Oh my God, this news station is so sensational, it's disgusting! Chloris flapped her wrists to convince the police and medics milling around that hers were as real as her sister's stiffening arms.

And so, in the space between life and death, between hope and misery, the mother had slipped away. When friends and neighbours handed consolatory bouquets to Chloris after the funeral reception, she began to regard life with suspicion. Likewise, Marilyn's insistence that Chloris bear no guilt added up to a growing thesis that their relationship must end, in the face of biological blood spilt on the connector road of her insipid trek. Her plan, her journey, her happiness. If you pushed too hard against the inevitable, harm would push back. The lurid blossoms provoked memory of the scent Charisma had liked to dab along the length of her braids before coiling them into her trademark loose chignon; lavish blue hydrangeas gradually desiccated to clumps the hue of dead lips. Like living alongside the crumpling up of a sign language. Night and day, refusing to answer Marilyn's phonecalls, rejecting the food she had asked friends to bring over, Chloris was saturated with memories of her sister's skin, her limbs, the way her hips had turned to follow the stretch of her shoulders while pulling canisters of dried goods from upper kitchen shelves, her burp-like laugh, her sullen, always reproachable silences. Why hadn't she known how to wait them out at a distance? Her concern for Cameo drew her back repeatedly to the cold front of her sister's rage. Chloris, no matter how cajoled by the ring of Marilyn's cunt, no matter how satiated her own smile in a mirrored bathtub soak, couldn't give up on knowing the child. And she wanted to believe that her sister's bias, no matter how convincingly deployed and stupid, was really just a protracted joke, underneath which simmered a bigness of heart that would, some day, reveal itself. If only, that is, she hadn't pushed.

Light years away, Cameo watched the yellow sky that night from a telephone booth in Coniston. I'll show her, she ranted in the pit of her lungs. No way to go home yet, not until her body was visibly changed by this self-designed rite of passage so that her mother's scolding would be useless. How dare she tell me who I can go out with, does she think I'm still a baby? Mr. Carter is a perfectly decent man. It's not like I'm having sex with him, or anything, I'm making out! That's what you're supposed to do when you're fourteen, Mom can just screw off! This was before drug rebellion and ideological revolt. Among the limited resources at her youthful disposal was Cameo's quite impressive ability to temporarily forsake. Food and water, love and attention, hearth and roof. When I'm good and ready, she thought, I'll go back. The patch of sky, which had been milky for a short time, cleared. Then the torrential rain began. Getting soaked to the skin was not the problem; it was the foreboding that she shouldn't have run out like that, that with her mother away her father would be needing her. She pushed a quarter in the pay phone and a stranger's voice, which turned out to be their neighbour, told her to come home immediately, refusing to explain. Cameo figured her father had fallen in the lake.

STEVEN HEIGHTON

On Earth As It Is

Father

Stavros learned that time does not so much dull a pain as seal it off, the way a membrane formed around the poisons in his father's gut after his appendix cracked open like an egg, and for a year nobody knew, not even his father, till the surgeons cut him open for something else and there it was. A lunar, bluish ball, wobbling and amniotic, it still seethed with poisons, though they were securely walled in and had done no obvious harm. But the doctors soon learned that the tumour they'd cut him open to remove was anything but harmless, and their gloved hands, palms turned up in attitudes of defeat, might have flittered helpless over the opened body like spirits escaping from the flesh.

Suppose that all doctors knew exactly where to pry; suppose that their eyes and their instruments were more acute than they are, more attuned. Surely on cutting into the body of a man or a woman they would find other organs like that, and the older the patient the more they would find. Could be that death comes in part because the sealed-up grief gradually crowds out and weakens every essential life-organ. Could be the membranes make an imperfect seal and they leak, they drip—like IV bags, but toxic— so a tincture of past sorrow is always circling in the blood.

Still, with age Stavros shut away the night of his father's death—he was only six at the time—and another night a few summers later when he was staying at a Greek Orthodox boys' camp up in the hill country north of Toronto. That night had always involved his father too, though his father had not been there. He was safe in the earth and he was up in the stars—so his mother and brothers had reassured him, often—but now their words were no consolation because at night, north of the city, the stars were shining fingertips that seemed close enough to touch, yet they were so cold, and far, and they did not touch back.

Our Father who aren't in heaven, that was how the first line of the prayer always sounded when they recited it at school each morning or in the camp chapel before breakfast. Anyway it was best to think of him safe in the earth—that was easier to think of, easier to believe. Easier to think of him rising out of the earth back into the world where people loved him than to picture him floundering down from the sky like some slingshot-shattered bird—or, in Stavros' nightmare, a bag of debris, discarded from a passing jet, split and spilling its rank, rotting contents as it tumbled back to earth.

Son

The boys, sweating, stumbled up a dark path cobbled with fist-sized stones and the boughs and unripe apples that had fallen in Sunday's gale. There was no moon. Up ahead clear of the trees a dozen flashlights flickered over the bare hill and the boys pressed on, shoving each other, swearing, loosing the odd clap of high-pitched laughter. It was hard to keep up with the counsellors. The priest would be up ahead too, scything through the tall grass with his massive strides, his long robes swirling around his ankles.

It's a perfect night for it, one boy whispered. The counsellors say it's perfect.

What do snipes look like anyway?

Nobody knows.

Your counsellor doesn't even know? What about Papa Yiannis?

Won't say, the boy whispered, louder. Be quiet now.

I don't see how we can catch them if we don't even—

Quiet! They're afraid of people—we've got to be quiet.

Sounds of laboured breathing as the boys climbed. The pulsing hum of late-summer cicadas in trees that could not be seen: a buzzing that seemed to flag and fizzle out as the boys pushed on, like the sound of a childhood toy, all but abandoned, the batteries almost dead.

I don't even believe in them, snipes.

Yeah? So what are those bags for?

A flashlight-beam up ahead had caught a green garbage bag and the fisted hand of the counsellor holding it. The boys were falling farther back.

Santa Claus carries a big bag too, said the skeptical boy. Him and the tooth fairy.

This is different.

QUIET, a counsellor called back, his flashlight wheelin at them like a single blazing eye.

Stavros was not sure what to think. His father had taught him a bit about birds and he thought he had heard of these snipes, but he seemed to remember they lived in marshes and along the sea. Still, he could not believe that Papa Yiannis and the counsellors would lead the whole camp into the hills for nothing on such a hot night. And dark—Stavros seemed to be wading through the dark like an astronaut outside his ship, line severed, limbs flapping, somehow hoping to find solid earth under his foot as he struggles. But only stars. Ahead of him a sudden bulking of shadow and he collided with something big; he was sworn at in Greek, he was shoved and crumpled back into the grass. He sat very still. The grass around him hissed like some living thing as the other boys rushed on. A good smell rose out of the earth—an odour of soil and wet clover, wildflowers, split apples—and he let himself glance up at the sky and pick out the clear constellations his father had taught him. No more than a few seconds passed, but by the time he scrambled to his feet the flashlights far ahead of him were swithering like fireflies, growing fainter and fainter.

As he ran he felt the ground level out and soon he caught up with the other boys, the counsellors, and Papa Yiannis. He could not actually see Papa Yiannis but he could hear his voice—firm, resonant, and reassuring—booming above him out of the dark.

Papa Yiannis was repeating what he had told them in the assembly hall a short while before: snipes were very fast and clever and the only way to catch them was on a moonless night because their eyesight was bad and they could not see you. But they had good ears and they could hear you even if you whispered so you had to be quiet—silent, absolutely—and you had to stick close by your counsellor. If you bent down and felt along the earth with your hands you might come across some snipes and you must squeeze them tight and hold them or they would run away. Snipes could not fly but they were fast on their feet.

The boys did their best in the dark to form up around their counsellors. Flashlight-rays strobed over the hilltop and were swallowed by the trees and the high grass, then a whistle shrilled and the boys, panting, giggling in staccato bursts and telling each other to shut up, scattered into the night. Something slithered across Stavros' path. He froze in mid-step. Something else rattled towards him and clunked into his ankle: a small rock snared and tossed away by one of the others.

Stavros knelt and stretched out his hands, palms open, feeling for the earth and timidly touching it like the rough black hide of some massive animal. Fallen dead, or just sleeping? He'd had dreams. The same irrestrainable urge to reach out, same tantalizing dread: cold pebbles, dank slimy stems, a thistle prickling under his hand, then his fingers squelching into something soft and pulpy and he gasped and pulled back as if the sick fox that two boys had cornered behind the chapel and beaten with lacrosse sticks a week before was up here on the hill, had crawled up here to die, its mashy wounds splayed under his hands. He sniffed: the tart cidery rankness of crushed apple.

He stood and tugged at the damp, rolled sleeve of his counsellor Petros to ask him about the snipes—was it true, were they really so fast? Petros craned the flashlight up at his own face and set a finger to his clamped lips. A glowing skull, eye-sockets caved and fathomless, leered down at Stavros and he jerked back and looked away, first into the dark around him, then up at the stars: the Bear, the Serpent, the Dragon. He thought again of his father, teaching him the names. His throat tightened.

Caught one! somebody cried and immediately the cry was echoed. An older boy in Stavros' group hooted in triumph and a darting flashlight beam caught him in silhouette, lowering his cupped hands into the counsellor's sack.

Chris, Stavros' only friend at the camp, lurched into him.

Caught anything?

Oh, Stavros breathed, it's only you.

What did you expect? The snipes can't hurt you.

I haven't caught any, Stavros said.

Me too. *Tipota.* . . .Are they real, do you think?

They must be, Stavros said gravely, why else would we be here?

SHHHH! Petros loomed above them. Again his face was deformed by the rising light, made ancient, like the racked features of saints in the icons of the camp chapel, candlelit from below. Here, the face ordered, feel the sack. At once they ran their hands over the bottom of the raised bag, Stavros sure he felt on his palm the prickling of tiny, clawed feet.

I felt them too! Chris said.

They begged Petros to shine his light into the bag so they could see the snipes, but Petros refused—bright light would stun the birds and wreck the boys' fun, later.

Anyways it's almost time to go, Petros said. The sacks are filling up.

Shouts of triumph from somewhere nearby. Stavros' eyes were getting used to the dark and now he made out Papa Yiannis—at least the pale skin of his face above his beard and below his cap—gliding towards them out of the fields. His long black robes were hissing, rustling invisibly in the grass.

Time to go back! he said in a large voice, teeth flashing in his beard. Have you caught many snipes?

I didn't catch any, Stavros blurted into the dark.

The skeptical boy snickered. Chris gave Stavros a poke in the ribs.

Now shut up, Petros said.

The assembly hall was even darker than the hills, and hotter. Stavros could no longer see the priest's face, though under the high ceiling his voice was clearer than ever, larger, more fatherly; but no longer reassuring. Stavros held himself stiffly on the damp bench, the other boys invisible to his right and, to his left, Petros: a mass of moving shadow exuding heat and a dense, sweaty smell. He wanted to reach out and tug at the young man's wrist, shown only by the ghost-glow of his diving watch. He wanted to ask what Papa Yiannis could possibly mean.

The instructions were simple enough. Apparently some of the other counsellors were up at the front before the lines of benches jittering with boys and when Papa Yiannis gave the word they would upend the garbage bags and free the snipes. But snipes run very fast (the priest's voice cut through the darkness) so the minute we empty the bags you must all start stamping up and down in place so that none may get away.

The dark hall was still and solemn. Stavros thought he caught from behind him a faint crackle of laughter, whispering, then silence. Petros breathing, calm and slow.

Jim the cook has promised to make us something nice of the birds for tomorrow.

More laughter, a few cries of alarm, disgust.

Snipe pie!

You are ready?

He looked around to find what the other boys were doing. The faces beside and behind him were pale circles, formless in the dark, like the hockey stars and framed saints above his bed whose features dimmed to anonymity when his mother flicked off the light. *Petro,* he whispered, but the young man did not respond. He was rising to his feet, Stavros sensed it. The other boys were rising too. A few of them chuckled and muttered softly. *Chris?* Stavros said, but his friend was not beside him.

ALL RIGHT, Papa Yiannis' voice rang out, LET THEM GO!

In seconds the tumult of shouting and laughter and the thunder of feet thumping the pine boards reached such a pitch that Stavros gave up calling his friend and just hunkered on the bench, curled into himself, feet clear of the floor. The bench quaked and swayed. For a second he felt sure it would tip and throw him under the feet of the howling boys, but he held on, a small thing trapped on the bough of a tree shaken from below. He peered into the darkness but saw no snipes. The awful pounding seemed to be inside him, gathering pace and strength, hammering out at his ribs and small chest.

The bench shuddered once more, swayed, and toppled.

Arms stretched and beating the air for balance Stavros fell straight back, tensing his body, but the floor was not there and he was falling for what seemed a long time as if a hole had opened in the earth and swallowed him. All sounds were muffled and the impact, when it finally came, was muffled too, and painless. Dark and still, like in the grass stargazing with his father on a summer night, but under the ground the stars are hidden. With him. In the night-sky of the earth.

The lights burst on and he shut his eyes against the glare and his hearing rushed back: the thumping was over but the roar of voices was louder now, discordant, a crossfire of disbelieving cries and smug, knowing laughter and disappointment and the skeptical boy could be heard sniggering and when Petros and the boys found Stavros and helped him up there were a few noises of concern.

Dazzling faces ringed him. You fell right under my feet, Petros said, eyes wide, his blanched face shoving in huge and close. You're all right?

THE SNIPES ARE ALL GONE, the priest boomed from the front of the hall, THEY ALL GOT AWAY. I AM AFRAID JIM LEFT THE SIDE DOOR OPEN AND THE BIRDS....

Jim, the old cook, stood sheepishly at the priest's side, his felt cap in his hands.

Boys, I'm sorry.

Everyone watched Jim and the priest, and Stavros was forgotten. His ribs and right forearm throbbed, his eyes stung, the kettle-drum beating that had ceased for others when the lights came on was still pounding in his chest. But his heart lifted as he scanned the floor by the toppled bench and saw nothing but gum wrappers and a crumpled leaflet from the morning service.

I can't believe it, the skeptical boy said, and nodded to show that in fact he could. Look it, check it out. He's still crying.

Chris was beside him. We hurt you when you fell?

He's all right, Petros said, and his arm coiled out along Stavros' shoulder and weighed it down. Just a bit shaken. Aren't you, Stavro?

It wasn't just that I fell.

HE'S ALL RIGHT, Petros announced, as if echoing words

Stavros had said too softly for others to hear. HE'S FINE!

The priest reared above them, lips bitten in his beard.

It wasn't just *falling,* Stavros said, glaring round at a pack of strangers. It wasn't! The skeptical boy pursed his mouth at him, shook his head. The sweating faces of the priest and counsellor loomed above the others and frowned down in confusion, concern. Suddenly Stavros saw it had all been a prank, he was the last to understand. His eyes filled, brimmed over, and the ring of faces dissolved.

Don't worry, Papa Yiannis, he'll be fine. Fine.

How can you be so sure?

Look, he's still crying, one of the boys said.

Did you know? Stavros, half blind behind tears, turned on his friend: You were stomping with the others! Did you know all along?

The friend leaned toward him and whispered, Not for sure, but I wasn't taking any chances.

Each year, the priest sighed, there is a child like this.

Ghost

With time Stavros sealed away that night, but it ruptured open years later when, after high school, he went to Greece to visit cousins he had never met and to place in the family plot a lacquered cedar box containing a coarse lock of his father's hair, along with his amber *koumboloi.* He had also brought over a number of old volumes his father had willed the cousins on his death. By this time Stavros had forgotten almost all of his Greek, but he could tell from pictures in two of the frail calf-bound books that one of them was about stars and the other about birds. Of course. His father had been a keen watcher of the skies and as a small boy Stavros had watched with him, always eager to follow his upstretched arm and pointing finger, to hear him pick things out—day-dove, starling, Orion the hunter—but then his father had died and with time, as his memory faded, the boy's interests had realigned themselves and he had forgotten most of what he'd heard. The constellations in the dry air above the Attic coast were as bright as any astronomer could ask, yet Stavros could recognize little now but Hercules, the Big Dipper, the Pleiades, Orion. As for birds, the coast teemed with them and the olive groves on the hills above the church and the graveyard bristled with busy nests, but Stavros felt only a vestigial interest—though for the sake of his father's memory, he tried to feel more.

Still, the night before he left his cousins for Athens and the flight home he was made to recall his boyhood fascination with birds, and to remember the snipes, and that night at the summer camp. He was walking alone by the sea, near the graveyard. The moon was almost full and a small island a mile offshore mirrored its light so richly, it seemed a second moon had plunged into the Aegean, only a sliver of it showing above the tide. Ahead, just up from the waterline, Stavros saw two small boys hunkered down, crawling or wrestling—or were they playing with something in the sand between them? As he approached they fell silent, then sprang apart whispering urgently, their repeated word clear: *Xenos*. A foreigner. Outsider.

The boys slouched, eyeing Stavros in the stumped, sullen manner of children who realize they've done something punishable but have no idea why others think it so wrong. They seemed to be awaiting his sentence, or absolution. Then at their feet Stavros made out something small and dark, something thrashing in the sand. At first he thought it was a crab they had buried deep in its own element, meaning no harm, then realized the waving leg was actually a wing. A head appeared, then the jerking neck of a small bird flapping itself free of the mud.

Stavros' feelings must have shown in his face. Before he could even snap the word *figé*—a simple command he still knew—the boys had turned and were darting away up the beach.

Stavros knelt in the dampness and clawed gently at the sand behind the bird's head. It cheeped sharply, twisting its tiny beak round at him to cast what seemed a stern, affronted look. He smiled and made a soothing noise in his throat, eyes smarting from the sand churned up by the sail-shaped wing. For a moment his scooping fingers pressed into the bird's back and he felt the heat of the damp body quivering through the down.

Then, although the bird still seemed half-buried, its other wing snapped loose and it shot up out of the hole, its wet, softly thudding wings flashing in the moonlight as it surged away over the beach, the shallows, the eggshell-sliver of island out to sea.

Emavora

The dying mother sent the two girls out of the room, and called in my father to entrust them to him. They were eighteen and twenty and, in their high heels, they topped him by a head (we were small in my family). He, at forty-two, had just been elected President of the Greek Community, and people were predicting he would be going places, which may have been why the mother called him to her bedside at a time like this—apart from the fact that she was not on speaking terms with any of her relatives. If you didn't have your choice of relatives, might as well pick a promising stranger.

She handed him the bonds and the policies. She had written to her sister in Greece, "a peasant," she apologized contemptuously. "Let her guard their virtue while you manage the money." And she winked, a wink my parents would decode together later, as a sure bet the sister, although estranged for thirty years, would gladly row across the Atlantic for the sake of her nieces' honour, and that unwooed and unwed herself, would relish nothing better than shooing suitors away like flies.

"I can't leave two grown daughters unchaperoned," the mother explained. "People would talk. You know how people are."

Father agreed, firmly.

It was then she issued her fateful warning. "Roula will be a handful—*emavora*," she hissed. And a curse for the younger daughter quickened her last breath. What she meant by *emavora*— not the etymology but what *she* meant—remained a secret between herself and Father. Maybe she never told even Father. Maybe even she didn't know. Maybe the word, correctly as she used it, loomed larger than any of us: a Pythian word not ours to decipher. Maybe only Roula could understand it, because no one else thirsted for blood, no one else would have recognized the taste.

"If the girl's so bad," Mother remarked later between pursed lips, "why wasn't she left to fare for herself instead of being dumped on you and the aunt?"

"Because you don't abandon your child, however bad," Father said sternly. "At least Greek mothers don't." This was a dig at Mother, who was not Greek, but who was not one to take a dig lying down either.

"Well and in this country, not only do mothers not abandon their children," she snapped, "they try not to talk against them to strangers."

My parents did not fight low. They jousted on tasselled chargers. They armed themselves with embroidered generalities that glittered with the gold of righteousness.

Roula's mother had died in the summer of her fiftieth year; and my parents now discussed her age at length because, after all the trouble she had taken to conceal it, there it was, big as life on her death certificate.

We children had never seen the deceased other than in V-necked black crepe. The very white, ample flesh of her face had been going a little slack by then; but the rest of her was surprisingly firm, down in the deep Vs. With her husband dead eight years, longer than I had been alive, she managed to maintain an attitude of fresh widowhood awash in tears like lobster in a saltwater tank, her habitual expression one of pungent and wet disappointment. Her husband's untimely death had stymied her ambitions. Now people whispered he had disappointed her in his lifetime too. And when I asked how—how had her husband disappointed her in his lifetime? Father answered with a Greek proverb of which he had enough to cover or evade any situation, while Mother concluded caustically: "It's a shame she never realized a smile is the cheapest facelift."

So Martha and Roula were orphans. I couldn't imagine a more tragic fate. The very word "orphan" made me weep, though at five-foot-eight the girls failed to fully release my flood-gates. Beside which they looked more lost than broken-hearted that summer, leaning on our porch banister in their chaste black clothes. Still, I managed a few tears out of loyalty to the word "orphan", especially for Martha who suffered from the heat and whom her mother had called a good-enough girl if only by comparison.

When the aunt arrived, we met her at the pier. She would have been impossible not to recognize. She was the mother's double but shorter, fatter, flabbier and older: last year's economy model of the very same line. She and Roula managed to clash immediately in the car between the boat and the girls' apartment.

"It's an insult!" Roula exclaimed with sobs in her voice (the aunt, who spoke only Greek, indicated by a wooden expression that she knew she was being talked about). "Typical of my mother to put her grown children at the mercy of some backward stranger she couldn't get along with herself!"

Father frowned. "You'll be good to your aunt."

"She's a busybody—"

"Of course she's a busybody," Mother said softly. "Isn't that what she's here for?"

"I don't want her living with us! She smells of garlic and mothballs. I'm going to boarding school."

"You are not," Father said. Martha had a job, but Roula was an honour student at university. "She'll look after the boy. Weekends, you'll come with us."

And so they did; the girls began visiting every Sunday. And true to his promise, Father made sure the aunt stayed home by simply not inviting the younger brother.

My sisters and I were subdued at first in the presence of such recent bereavement. I remember mysterious conversations downstairs after they left and after we were put to bed, when my parents switched over to Greek—but not always, because Mother's Greek was not concise enough for gossip—and when their secretiveness only forced us to exercise greater ingenuity. I have no doubt that had sex magazines been fashionable then, and had my parents ever bought one, and had they taken the trouble to hide it, I would have found it as I found everything in the end, including the prophylactics in a black and orange box, which (until I opened it) I thought contained tiny Turkish Delights because it had a silhouette of a minaret on the cover. I didn't like Turkish Delights. But these had to be very special indeed if Father took the trouble to hide them under his socks. I remember looking up from the open box, puzzled and guilty, straight into the eyes of a picture of Saint Joseph holding his lily on the wall.

Father loved the chaste Joseph—an unlikely choice of patron for a Greek non-Catholic, and a choice not exempted from my mother's jibes. Was he hoping to acquire elusive virtues by osmosis, she taunted? Was it the size of the shrine which impressed him? Or the fact that anyone with a dome so majestic had to have been a big shot? Of course in Greece, a cuckold, even a saint, was not much revered. But this was Canada, and Canadian men didn't fuss about honour: maybe a little immigrant in need of connections might do worse than worship somebody immensely influential here?

Whatever his reasons, and perhaps also because a visit to the Oratory was free, we all traipsed over to call on Saint Joseph almost every Sunday afternoon. Climbing on foot the steps the pilgrims climbed on their knees, I sometimes ran ahead, and then paused and pretended to be a real pilgrim myself. But I knew I might as well pretend to be a chartered accountant. And I knew dimly too that if they had a secret password, my non-Catholic father would sooner possess it than I.

Since Martha and Roula came along on our excursions, we made a ritual of lighting a lampion for their mother. The heart of Brother André, founder of the shrine, floated in a jar of preservative like a colloidal suspension. Crutches dangled in the blinking light. I no longer had to rake my head for a miracle to pray for: I prayed for the resurrection of the girls' mother. I imagined her rising all of a sudden between the crutches and the lampions, maybe someone else was in her grave, maybe she had been alive all the time. I imagined Martha crying "*Manoula!*" and bursting into tears while Roula, passionately repentant, renounced her blood thirst forever; and sobbing, and freshly widowed, and orphaned, and then restored to each other again, they all descended on our house to *stay*, and shipped the aunt right back to Greece.

After viewing the heart, we usually crossed over to the Wax Museum luncheonette for an ice cream cone. I wish I could report here that Roula often or even just once chose strawberry, and that bites of the fruit clung to her lips like blood clots. But either she didn't, or I don't remember.

The first winter of the girls' mourning seems to have been rich in weddings and christenings. While clashes with the aunt caused Mother to declare Euripides should have been there taking notes, Father, as President of the Community, was often called upon to serve as best man or godfather. We were old enough to drag along. The girls needed distractions. "Once we've paid for a present,"

Father murmured mischievously, "might as well get as many free meals as we can out of that wedding, eh?"

Greek sacraments were lavish affairs where it was *mal vu* not to make a display of sentiments. Parents walked their daughters to the altar with torrents of tears dripping on their shoes. Babies even old enough to swim reacted to the baptismal fonts as if they had been tossed in boiling oil. And widows refused tranquilizers so as to howl more convincingly.

In this tradition, inevitably, Roula made a bad impression. People who remembered her dry-eyed at her mother's funeral now observed her coldness of heart towards her aunt. It was rumoured she would be hard to find a husband for. The name "*Emavora*" even leaked out.

"She's being ostracized," Father sighed one evening at the dinner table, long after the rest of us had eaten supper in the kitchen.

"No wonder," Mother said a little tartly. "Anyway is it usual to invite people to parties when their mother's just died? How can Martha and Roula have time for anybody else, the way we're monopolizing them? Why don't we leave them alone for a while and see if they get invited elsewhere? It can't be fun for two young girls to be with a married couple and three small children all the time."

"You don't understand our customs," Father sighed. "Greek girls don't run around the way you North Americans do. Their mother entrusted them to me. And as you know," he paused for effect, or for an allusion to sink in (one I had missed), or maybe only to take another bite, "I am not the one to take my responsibilities lightly."

So if we went anywhere *en famille*, that winter, we went with the girls, and as usual we went on a whim. My father was all for doing things when and if he felt like it. As a result, and in spite of the fact that he considered himself responsible, and quite rightly so, he treated RSVP's as if they were for other people. Bills he was never nonchalant enough to leave unpaid. But RSVPs he was not yet socially scrupulous enough to deal with before the last minute. Years later, I would realize I had learned to tell the newcomers from the natives by simply watching them open their mail: they had different priorities, what they took seriously said it all.

Once he had decided that, yes, we were going to this one, he would phone the girls. "How about a wedding this afternoon?"

Mother scampered to his side, waving her arms: "For heaven's sake, they're not invited!"

"They're not invited, eh?" Father repeated, winking at the receiver while she went into a silent dance beside him. "I don't see that this invitation specifies NO CHILDREN...?"

"They're not children and they're not ours!" Mother whispered convulsively. "Even Greeks don't invite their friends to other people's weddings!"

"My wife believes she's an expert on Greek manners," Father chortled. "Never mind what she says. We'll pick you up at four. I take it you'll be ready and not keep us waiting."

If Martha was on the line, the conversation ended there. If Roula had picked up the call, however, there was likely to be a pause when she snapped: "Well and don't *you* keep us waiting either," because Father would add: "*I* will keeping you waiting if I have to. But *you* will not keep *me* waiting," before he hung up, much amused.

In silence—and not necessarily strict silence—I always rooted for Father. Mother could be fun when she was in charge, but she didn't overpower circumstance the way he did. Nor was she sure enough of herself to be entirely loyal. With Father on your side, you were a winner. With Mother, it was touch and go. Furthermore, when Father took it upon himself to be Fun, she had to slip into a No Fun position if only for the sake of maintaining a balance. Yet she was not allowed to be Fun when he played No Fun.

I had also noticed that while Father's presence seemed to heighten Roula's sense of humour, Roula's presence seemed to deaden Mother's. Again, I supposed, a matter of balance.

So Mother inherited the bum role in a family group. She couldn't match Father, and half the time she didn't want to, and she couldn't beat him either. All she could do was register protest. Endlessly.

The crunch came when an invitation did specify NO CHILDREN.

"No children, eh?" Father grinned, mischievous, while Mother tried in vain to dissuade him, and we denounced her for siding with strangers against us, and Roula goaded him on: "Yeah, isn't old man Gavaris a sourpuss and a cheapskate!"

"What will you do to him if he kicks me out?" I would ask her, delighting in advance in the ferocity of her answers. Roula dared take anyone on, even a man, even an old one, even at his own daughter's wedding. "Even her own mother," my mother had to remind me: "She isn't *Emavora* for nothing."

Old man Gavaris (or Nakis, or Maroulis, or Kouloukoundis) invariably seemed surprised but delighted to see us, not one inch the sourpuss described some hours earlier. "Your invitation specified NO CHILDREN, but—" my father would point out as if it were necessary, as if we were not visible behind him, ogling the buffet table: "I brought mine anyway."

"When I specified NO CHILDREN," our host would retort unctuously, "I did not mean that you, my friend, could not bring along yours. Your children are my children." And turning to the girls: "I see he takes his responsibilities very much to heart."

Later, I would catch him glowering at our group while mumbling remarks which I imagined a lot less flowery. Meeting my eye, he would rush over. He would ask: was I being a good girl? And I would nod: "*Mallista*", hoping he believed I'd understood every word, which of course I hadn't. And I knew he knew I hadn't. It was common knowledge among Greeks that my father's children didn't speak the language—what else could you expect with him married to "that foreigner"? My mother's ancestors may have landed here three hundred years ago; but the fact earned her no greater regard, from Montreal Greeks, than what the Indians had got from the French when they first arrived.

Father mystified me, around that time, with vague allusions to "the sins of the fathers".

"What sins?" I asked, frankly unimpressed by Greek Orthodox sins, because if Father's religion wasn't the true religion, how could his sins be true sins?

He puzzled me even more by his reaction to my report that every time I missed school, the whole class fell on its knees to pray for his conversion. "Do you know what Catholic means?" I had added, laying a pious trap for him.

He didn't bother answering. He just remarked with quiet and troubled humility that if the nuns were going to pray for his soul, they ought to know he was facing worse problems than mere semantics.

"What are semantics?" I asked, sidetracked.

Mother entered the room at that moment, and he put a finger to his lips. I walked away assuming semantics must be heretics of some sort.

When he alluded to "the sins of the mothers," however, my eyes popped: "Not Mother too!"

"Not your mother," he said. "The girls' mother. Roula's. I'm beginning to wonder if she didn't know this would happen. If she didn't want it to, maybe even planned it..."

They were still visiting on Sundays, with or without excuses of aunt, mourning, weddings or christenings. Most times, they simply joined us for lunch, or when we lunched out, tagged along. Father would meet them at church, drive the boy and the aunt home, and then return with the two girls. We were welcome to accompany him to his church anytime, as long as we didn't miss our own compulsory Mass which had the one advantage of being short.

The Orthodox service was an event: social, sumptuous and interminable. Greeks used incense lavishly. They sang more, louder and better, and had wonderful harmonies. They gave out food—cake-like breads on certain feasts, and steamed sweetened grain decorated with almonds, raisins and silver nonpareils at anniversary services. They allowed hordes of lively children to run around. They sold candles of every size in the vestibule, some for setting in candelabra, others for holding, which they didn't hesitate to put in the unsteady hands of babies. How fire never broke out must have been a proof of God's watchful presence; though I wonder why, if He could stop that kind of conflagration, He allowed the other kind to rage unchecked. It wasn't as if there had been no appeal. Most Sundays, we ended up going to church three times: to the Catholic Mass, to the Greek service, and then to Saint Joseph's Oratory. Was that not in itself a subconscious plea? An effort to ward off temptation? Or had all those visits to so many sanctuaries become no more than more occasions for falling?

The aunt returned to Greece for mysterious reasons, one of which was that her visa would not be renewed, another that the situation with Roula had deteriorated beyond all expectations, and a third and even more intriguing: that she wasn't on speaking terms with Father. He reported all this, leaving a great deal unsaid, in an injured voice where I detected a measure of falseness. I suspected he knew why the aunt had turned on him. He'd never for his part made any pretence of liking her. So why did he now feign surprise by her bad faith, as he put it?

The Sundays followed Sundays, and the girls reappeared like perennials. And we never knew where we would end up for lunch until long past noon, when Father and his compeers had filed out of church, and determined not whose turn it was to entertain, but what was on the menu at each man's house. While Father eagerly forsook beef or chicken for lamb, I suspected that for the more exotic dishes, the ones Mother couldn't or wouldn't prepare, he might have relinquished his very right of primogeniture. For *barbounia* with their heads on, for instance. For heads of anything that swam, flew, crawled or walked. For eyes and tongues and tails and feet and gizzards. A delicacy I remember going out for, among others, was lambs' testicles. Roula's delight on that occasion reached a paroxysm, while Mother, morosely, lunched on potatoes.

It was summer again, and we were spending July at a small hotel on the lower Saint Lawrence south shore where Father joined us on weekends. Right from the first, he brought the girls along. They towered over us in their white shorts, displaying lengths of fuzzy young legs, and I was already observant enough to find the contrast unkind with Mother's thin, blue-veined ones. But I didn't dare warn her. Mother resented criticism almost hysterically, and those death curses were recent enough to make anyone eager to be a favourite daughter. Still, I wished I might have been allowed to point out white shorts were sexier than white socks, knits than blouses, sandals than loafers. The list of what was sexy and what wasn't seemed pretty clear to me. How come I knew, the girls knew, Father might notice, yet she, Mother, didn't have a clue?

The clues were piling up.

I remember a party for Roula at our house, one Sunday after church, and Father's birthday gift: a navy blue silk robe in a style more appropriate for Mother—he must have sent her out to buy it. I remember how it rose from the tissue like a puppet, very limp, very new, and how Roula held it against herself: "It's too small for me, Kostas!" (Father's name in Roula's voice rings through those years of my childhood.)

He helped her into the robe as if it were a coat. The sleeves barely covered her elbows. She threw her head back and abandoned herself to laughter, showing the insides of her mouth and nose in a frenzy of delight at once girlish and voracious. Father scampered around her, very amused, very animated I remember thinking: he's making a fool of himself. I turned to Mother to see how she was taking it. I was shocked. She was being by far the greater fool of the two. She just stood there, splitting her sides as if she had intended to ridicule Roula and as if, of all things, she believed she had succeeded. Why you only had to look at Father to know she hadn't! You only had to follow his shining eyes, to see Roula as he saw her: Roula dwarfing the rest of us, Roula soaring out of that skimpy robe, soaring and roaring like a goddess!

Late one afternoon, maybe of the same day, maybe of another Sunday, I remember dusk in the bay window of the livingroom, and the remains of a party smelling of damp ashes. I remember Father's arms around me, and my eyes closing. Voices wavered as my consciousness drifted, until a phrase emerged, assumed a shape. Something must have alerted me, maybe a peal of laughter, maybe a silence, maybe the fact it was Father speaking almost in my ear, as if he meant the words not only for me, yet for me *also*. Had he squeezed my shoulder? Had he called my name? Or was he only pretending to address me while addressing someone else?

"All men are the same," he said. Hardly an original statement.

We didn't shy away from Great Truths in my family. The trick was to unravel the particular from the general.

"All men are the same..." And an intense silence responded across the room. I forget who else was there. Or how I guessed he had paused to stare. By the tone of his voice? By a twitch of his arm? By a catch in his breath? I felt too sleepy to open my eyes. Besides, in a way, I saw better without looking. I knew that what he directed at me was the excuse, the apology, the warning. What I didn't know was who else he spoke the words for. What else they meant. Or how vividly I would remember them. How profoundly they would shape me, years later.

Martha and Roula had become a part of our family. Anytime we received an invitation, Father would ask in a soft voice: "May we bring the girls along? They have been entrusted to me, you know. I don't like to abandon them on a Sunday noon," (or on a Saturday night, or on an Easter morning, or on a summer weekend).

It was clear Roula enjoyed our company: I'm sure she never had to be coaxed. But what about Martha? Was she really the shadowy figure I remember, eclipsed by her more stellar sister? Or could it be she was fed up with us?

And what about the younger brother? It seems strange to me now that we could have made such a fuss about his sisters, and yet ignored him so consistently. Where did he spend his Sundays after the aunt returned to Greece? Who had he been entrusted to?

Anyway, just when it seemed we could do nothing, go nowhere anymore without the girls, Martha dropped out. She had a boyfriend.

"Is he a good boy?" Mother asked one night when Father dined alone in the dining-room as was his recent habit.

He shrugged. "How would I know." He took another bite. He

added without conviction: "Martha's being difficult."

"Pardon?"

"Difficult."

She slipped him a sharp look. "Shouldn't you look into it?"

He sighed. "It isn't my business."

"You promised the mother."

"It's not so simple. The girl is of age. I've turned over her assets to her. She didn't ask me to continue to look after them, so I won't."

Mother stared at him across the table. She ate earlier, with us. He was always late, a festive presence becoming rare, though not as rare as a year from now. She was wearing a dark skirt, a pale blue cardigan over a white blouse and, as usual, socks and loafers. She had just had her hair cut again, too short. She was tailored as opposed to glamorous or sexy. Her attitude was tailored, too.

"You surprise me, Kostas," she said. "You seem relieved to be rid of Martha. I would have expected you to be much more protective, more strict with a young girl."

He continued to eat, gazing at her with his mouth full. She was forever making fun of his large mouth, of his appetite. He filled the silence now with a sound of chewing, and a look passed across my mother's eyes which I knew well, a look of irony and contempt.

She said: "I would have expected Roula to get a boyfriend first."

"Why?"

"She's so much more rebellious and outgoing. But of course if she did, she'd be sneaky enough not to tell you."

Father's eyes focused sharply. "No," he said with his mouth full. "Roula has no boyfriend."

"How do you know?"

"I know," he said.

Strange things happened after that.

Father got a relapse of an old illness. Chills racked him, knocked the teeth in his mouth and banged the bed board on the wall. "Malaria," Mother murmured sinisterly: "A parasite." And she evoked Greece which she called the Near East, with an air at once bewildered and disdainful. Olives grew on trees over there. People ate octopus. Soldiers wore *skirts*. And when the Bulgars had invaded a village, they'd cut the priest in little pieces and thrown him in the well, thus depriving populations of both their leaders and their water.

Father demanded Roula be summoned to his bedside. She was familiar with the disease, she would know what to do. But it was obvious to me she wasn't and didn't. I remember her standing by the bed, as puzzled as we. And Father slipping her crass, sidelong glances as if there were two of him: one sick and shaking, and another one not sick at all, hiding underneath.

One night, he seemed so ill, mother dashed out in her negligee to get the help of another Greek who lived above his restaurant two blocks down the hill. I ran out after her—Father must have sent me. I forget whether I stopped her. Or if the man came over. All I remember is a sense of urgency, an image of my mother running over the white cement sidewalk with her black transparent negligee flying behind her. I'd stared at her in disbelief before she ran out. I'd never seen her wearing such a garment. It had a Peter Pan collar and short puffy sleeves—as though she'd tried to look sexy for once, and then changed her mind. You couldn't look sexy or mysterious in a thing like that. You could only look desperately available and very aware that you were nude.

I last remember Roula with us on a Sunday afternoon towards the end of summer. Belmont Park didn't seem seedy then, the rides didn't give me a headache, the loudspeakers weren't as loud, you could hear the motorboats on the river, and the river lapping the shore, and people on the roller-coaster, screaming.

Father's eyes were very green, very piercing, that day. "Who's for the roller-coaster?" he asked. The surprise would have been if Mother had cried, "Me!" which, of course, she didn't.

My two sisters and I fitted into one seat, while Roula got in with Father behind us. When we emerged from the tunnel before the climb up the first hill, I turned around and noticed how flushed they were. When we plunged down the other side, I heard her screaming. And when at last my sisters and I stumbled out, almost too weak with fear to walk, Father and Roula stayed on for two more turns.

Mother's mood deteriorated. She was snapping. Nagging. Refusing to have fun. Incurring our indignation by demanding we go home. At once. And, of course, wearing those awful white socks.

My brother was born in November. I didn't know about pregnancy. No one had told me.

Late one afternoon, Mother sat in her bedroom rocking the boy, her first after three girls, a cause for rejoicing, but Father didn't even come home to dinner these days. The blinds were down, or the sun, or both. As she rocked, her face appeared in the light from the hall, and disappeared, and reappeared again a moment later.

"Your father has a girl friend," she said.

I waited for the light to catch the glisten on her cheek. I hoped I had been wrong, that this might be a joke. But no, it wasn't.

I asked: "Who?" I knew very well who.

"Guess," she said, our eyes meeting in the light, her liquid eyes coming at me before they toppled backwards.

It wasn't much of a riddle. I guessed wrong on purpose so

she wouldn't know how noticeable it had been.

"Come on," she insisted. "You can do better than that."

So I said: "Okay. Roula," because I didn't want to appear stupid, either.

"Are you shocked?" she asked me from the darkness.

How could I be shocked by something which had happened little by little under my very nose? I answered: "No."

She sighed and sniffled and hung her head in shame. The chair creaked to a stop. She was crying freely now. I drew close. I slipped an arm around her shoulders. I felt her solitude, her sense of uniqueness. As if no husband had ever betrayed a wife before. As if she had a copyright on humiliation. As if it took a special kind of monster to inflict this upon her. And she spoke the monster's name suddenly, with such raw hatred that the baby started to cry. I said: "Shh." I smelled on her breath a perfume without flowers. I wondered what an *emavora*'s breath would smell like. I didn't even wonder what *emavora* meant anymore. I must have thought I finally understood.

On the other hand, we should not fall into the equally dangerous trap of romanticizing the Greeks as some perennially strange people, who reveal their truest and darkest souls in passionate outbursts on rooftops, late at night with a full moon beaming down.

–Christopher Faraone, *Ancient Greek Love Magic*

Family Tree

1
Grandmother owned acres
of common opinion
cursing the misfortune
of daughter after daughter.

Mother, for a dowry
got 90 limitations
dutifully displayed them
and promised them to me.

Peter gets the house
when Mom and Dad die.
I get what is lurking
in the hope chest
with the bedding.

2
Father, like Plato, held
in his mind a world of ideal things,
solutions exact in their symmetry,
universal truths without deviations.

Merciless, he criticized the food
my mother made. He fantasized ideal meals,
noodles salted perfectly, textures
found only in dreams.

Mother spoke low Greek, could not
recite the ancients. She dirtied her hands
with realities, gave birth three times,
and improvised our daily bread.
Mother cooked a lifetime of imperfect
meals, but still we grew up strong.

3
Daughters of immigrants, we
weren't taught to think big.
We were taught instead to do
many little things in order. Methodical
fathers said, don't spend money
you don't have. Sacrifice to pay off
a mortgage. Get a house, a husband, a yard
for the children. We were taught early,
eyes on the goal, taught to follow,
never to stray.

Our mothers came to this country
with nothing, one torn suitcase only.
Now they all have bungalows or more.
Tend, they say, your home, your garden.
Shun the wilderness of dreams, the gleam
of fools' ambitions, staggering risks
no girl should take.

We do things in small steps, gain small
satisfactions. We keep our doubts to ourselves.
Our poetry is prosaic. Daughters
of immigrants, we are trying
to take the danger out.

Vanishing Greece

It's beautiful, our motherland. The old songs
for example, and the way they lift a bride
onto a white horse. The air was
clean in the villages, and no one set
an alarm. Daughter, it was better there. I can
say this honestly.

None of us made it to high school. Most of us
couldn't read. But we were sharp, we were
smart, there were no imbeciles
among us. By the tree where Maria was hanged,
the school kids used to chatter. We were poor,
without shoes. But we were happy.
I only remember happy.

I remember Nitsa's son, killed by
an angry horse, thrown, foot trapped in the
stirrup, dragged to death. We gathered by
Maria's tree and sang the dirges
adults sang. The bell rang in our little
church. Icons of Jesus
and Mary suffering, candles
burning silent.

How many examples do you need? The
motherland was like a poem. Listen, daughter and
record this miracle: all I remember is happy.

Glossary

agapé : love
barbouni(a) : mullet(s)
efharisto : thank you
emavora : bloodthirsty
erotiari : loverboy
fasaria : trouble, fuss
figé : leave, scram
galaktoboureko : flaky, cream-filled pastry
karpouzi : watermelon
komati : piece
koumboloi : worry beads
laterna : Greek barrel piano
lemonathes : sodas
lera : dirt, scum
malaka : wanker
mallista : yes, of course
manouli(a) : little mama(s)
megali : big
mikri : little
mou : my
mousmoula : medlar
moustaki : moustache
narghile : waterpipe, hookah
nero : water
opa : exclamation of joy or surprise
pida : jump
pordi : fart
re : you (slang)
tavli : backgammon

tipota : nothing
xenes : foreigner
yiayia : grandmother

Biographical Notes

Pan Bouyoucas was born in Lebanon of Greek parents from the island of Leros and Alexandretta (Turkey). He came to Canada in 1963. His first novel, *Le Dernier souffle*, was published in 1975; his most recent, *L'Autre* (2001), was a finalist for the Governor General's Award for Fiction and the Prix Marcel-Couture du Salon du Livre de Montréal. He is also an award-winning playwright and translator.

Margaret Christakos, a second-generation Greek-Canadian whose grandparents came from small villages in the Laconia region, was born and raised in Sudbury, Ontario, and since 1987 has lived in Toronto. She has published five collections of poetry and one novel, *Charisma* (Pedlar Press, 2000), which was shortlisted for the Trillium Book Award in 2001. She holds a BFA from York University and a MA in History and Philosophy of Education from OISE. She taught Creative Writing at the Ontario College of Art and Design from 1992 to 1997. She currently works at PEN Canada where she coordinates the Readers and Writers literary program.

Tess Fragoulis's first book, *Stories to Hide from Your Mother* (Arsenal Pulp, 1997) was nominated for the QWF Best First Book Award, and was recently translated into French. Her novel, *Ariadne's Dream* (Thistledown, 2001) was nominated for the 2003 IMPAC International Dublin Literary Prize. She has written for film, television, radio and newspapers in Canada, and has taught writing at Concordia University. Her current project is a novel set in 1920s Greece and Asia Minor (excerpted in this anthology). Born in Greece, her cultural background is a volatile mix of Cretan and Greek Macedonian. She is the first granddaughter of the acclaimed Cretan writer, Constantine Fragoulis.

Steven Heighton is the author of the bestselling novel, *The Shadow Boxer* (a *Publishers' Weekly* Book of the Year for 2002). His work is translated into several languages and has been nominated for the Governor General's Award, the Trillium Award, a Pushcart Prize, and Britain's W.H. Smith Award (Best Book of the Year). He has also won a number of awards, most recently the 2002 Petra Kenney Prize. Anansi published *The Address Book*, a new collection of poems in 2004. He is the 2004 Jack McClelland Writer-in-Residence at the University of Toronto. His mother's family came from Tripoli, in Peloponnesus.

Hélène Papachristidis Holden's father was born in Macedonia, in Eleftheropolis, City of the Free, though his family came from Epiros. Her grandmother, Eleni Saraidaris, was at one time the directress of all school teachers in Macedonia, and also wrote poetry. Hélène was named after her, albeit in French, because her mother is Québecoise. Holden has written four novels, several short stories, TV scripts, and one major film script. She has also performed her own monologue, *Take a Canadian Author to Bed Tonight*. In 1995 she received the Order of Canada.

Antonios Maltezos was born in Montreal. His parents emigrated from the island of Aegina into the heart of the Greek community—Park Extension. It was there where he first started to hear all the wonderful stories of life in the village. He writes as often as his three youngish children will allow.

Una McDonnell has performed her work at readings and music festivals, on top of café tables (to get a gig), and on one occasion in a boxing ring (she won her round). She attended the 2002 Banff Wired Writing Studio and has published poetry in *Arc* and *Prairie Fire*. Her Greek family name is Haronitis; her relatives are scattered across Greece and North America.

Helen Stathopulos is a librarian and a writer based in Toronto. She has published poetry in *Fireweed*, *The Malahat Review,* and *dig*. She also spent a few years as a quarterly contributor to the late, great C.U.N.T. zine. A Toronto Arts Council Grant has bought her time to complete a first collection of poetry. She traces her Greek origins to a few sleepy villages in the southwestern Peloponnesus. Usually she just says, "you know, near Kalamata."

Aliki Tryphonopoulos is currently completing a Masters Degree in Creative Writing at Concordia University in Montreal. Her work has been previously published in *The Backwater Review*. Her Greek heritage comes from her father, who was born in Methoni, a village in Messina.

Helen Tsiriotakis is a first-generation Greek-Canadian of Cretan heritage. She was born in Toronto, where she currently lives. She has also lived and worked in Hania, Crete. Her first collection of poetry, *A House of White Rooms* (Coach House Books), was shortlisted for the Pat Lowther Memorial Award in 2002. Her poetry was featured in the jazz suite, *Decoding: Dancing and Dreaming,* by composer Tim Posgate. She holds an English Specialist Hon. B.A. from the University of Toronto. She is currently at work on a novel.

Stavros Tsimicalis is a poet, restaurateur and chef. He was born in Skoura, a village by the Eurotas River in Laconia, and arrived in Canada in 1963. He is the author of three books of poetry:

Exiled the Myth Needles Deeper (Porcupine's Quill, 1982.) *Liturgy of Light* (Aya/Mercury Press, 1986), and *The Fragments* (Porcupine's Quill, 2002). Stavros Tsimicalis lives in Richmond Hill, Ontario with his wife, Mary, and their three daughters. He owns and operates Café Pleiade in Toronto.

Eleni Zisimatos Auerbach was born and raised in Montreal. Her family is originally from Kefalonia, the birthplace of her great great-grandfather, enlightenment poet, Andreas Laskaratos. She has published work in Canadian and US journals, some of which include *The Antigonish Review, The Fiddlehead, Matrix, Spire* and *Descant.* She was a finalist for two Irving Layton Awards in poetry and fiction at Concordia University, where she recently completed her second MA degree in Creative Writing. She is co-editor of the poetry journal *Vallum.* Her chapbook, *Summations: Travels through Italy,* is available from above/ground press.

Further Reading

Kamboureli, Smaro. *Scandalous bodies: Diasporic Literature in English Canada*; Don Mills : Oxford University Press Canada, 1999.

Kamboureli, Smaro, editor. *Making a Difference: Canadian Multicultural Literature*; Toronto : Oxford University Press, 1996.

Kamboureli, Smaro. "A Palidromic Journey: Eyeing the Greek Immigrant Journey." In *Proceedings of the First International Congress on the Hellenic Diaspora from Antiquity to Modern Times.* Editor: J.M. Fossey. McGill University Monographs in Classical Archaelogy and History, No. 10. Vol 2. Amsterdam: Gieben, 1991.

Klironomos, Martha. "Literature by Writers of Hellenic Origin in Canada: An Overview." *Women Writers of the Greek Diaspora: Proceedings.* Editors: Helen Nickas and Marianna Spanaki. Athens: Publication of the General Secretariat for the Greeks Abroad, 2001.

Klironomos, Martha. "The Poetics of Belonging: The Topos of 'Home' in Smaro Kamboureli's Journal 'in the second person.'" *Women Writers of the Greek Diaspora: Proceedings.* Editors: Helen Nickas and Marianna Spanaki. Athens: Publication of the General Secretariat for Hellenes Abroad, 2001.

Véhicule Press

www.vehiculepress.com